Mail Order Destiny

Book Five of
Mail Order Bluebonnet Brides

Charlotte Dearing

Author's note: I write clean, wholesome love stories set in late 19th century Texas. When I wrote this book, the fifth book of the Mail Order Bluebonnet Brides Series, I expected it to be the last book of the series. Along the way, I fell in love with Caleb, and I had to write his love story.

Caleb and Ginny's story is included at the end.

I hope you enjoy.

Chapter One

Sophia McSweeney

Sophia felt herself gritting her teeth more and more tightly with every step. She was on her way to see Mrs. Prescott, Boston's most well-known marriage broker.

A few days ago, she'd told Mrs. Prescott quite firmly that marriage to a stranger was impossible, especially one who wrote letters that hinted at destiny. Josh Bentley, the Texas rancher who clearly regarded himself quite highly, had the gall to suggest that their union was part of a bigger plan. Sophia had no faith in the plans of mortal men, or in their ability to see and understand God's plan, even when it hit them square in the face.

And besides, she was sure that God was too busy for the likes of her.

Yet, there she was, storming down the street to beg for a chance to wed Josh Bentley, a man who wrote letters with ridiculous notions. Sophia prided herself on her level-headed mind. She refused to think of anything so far-fetched. Normally. But her situation was not normal.

The sound of a plaintive voice stopped Sophia in her tracks.

Sophia had been so deep in thought, she'd almost forgotten about her dearest friend, trying her best to keep up. Virginia, or Ginny as she was called at the orphanage, was the reason Sophia needed to accept the mail-order bride offer.

Sophia retraced her path back to Ginny. It wasn't the girl's fault that she couldn't keep up, not with her delicate constitution. A childhood injury had left her prone to severe pains in her legs.

"I'm sorry," Sophia said as she came to Ginny's side. "I'm eager to speak to Mrs. Prescott and tell her I've changed my mind. In my haste, I'd forgotten all about you."

Ginny's lips tugged upwards. Sophia's breath caught in her throat and she could hardly help giving the girl an answering smile. Despite everything, little Ginny could always summon a smile. In the bleakest of days, living under the orphanage director's oppressive rules and harsh punishments, Ginny always kept a cheerful countenance.

"You see," Ginny gently teased. "I can't possibly go with you to Texas. You'll just forget me and lose me somewhere along the way." Her smile faded. An earnest expression came over her girlish features, making her look older than her fifteen years. "That's why you must go without me."

"Don't be silly. Josh Bentley made it perfectly clear he would never forgive me if I left you behind."

Ginny gaped. "You never said that he mentioned *me* in his letters."

Sophia knit her brow and fended off the twinges of her guilty conscience. She was lying. She didn't lie for her own gain, but sometimes resorted to lying to help others, especially Ginny. To keep her safe, it was, at times, a necessary evil.

"He did, in fact," Sophia said airily. "Many times. I must have forgotten."

After what happened that morning, the only thing that mattered to Sophia was to protect Ginny. Several street thugs tried, yet again, to lure the innocent Ginny into their crime ring. They'd cornered her on the street and demanded she join in on their thieving. Sophia had pulled the girl from danger and told the boys off, threatening them with dire consequences if they didn't heed her warnings.

The boys ran off, laughing. Sophia knew the time had come for her and Ginny to leave Boston.

A carriage, drawn by a pair of matched grays, came around the corner, wheels clattering over the cobbled street. The driver sneered at her and drove through the nearby muddy puddle. Sophia moved without thinking, shielding the younger girl from the cold splash of water. The icy water soaked her boots and cloak hem.

Ginny knit her brow. "You shouldn't have done that. You need to look your best if you hope to be a bride someday soon. Besides, I'm not made of spun glass."

Sophia dismissed her words. Ginny was delicate, and too thin, and took ill anytime a storm blew through. Sophia hardly cared about her own appearance.

The very last thing she wanted was to look her best. Ever since she turned fifteen, and had blossomed with curves she didn't want, she'd hidden any semblance of beauty that she had. Now that she was eighteen, she was older and wiser and considered herself quite adept at concealing any hint of feminine charms.

Sophia took Ginny's hand and led her down the street. "Just another block and we'll be there. You're to sit outside while I talk to Mrs. Prescott."

They stopped at a fruit stand and Sophia bought a shiny, red apple. She handed it to Ginny who took it with a grateful look.

"What about you?" the girl asked.

"I'm not hungry."

Ginny scoffed. "I don't believe you. Where did you get the money?"

"I earned it, delivering some letters for Mrs. Prescott."

"Of course, you did." Ginny took a dainty bite of the apple.

"Ask me no questions, and I'll tell you no lies."

Sophia diverted her eyes from Ginny. The truth was, she lied to Ginny again, and it wouldn't be the last time.

"Pickpocket," Ginny muttered. "Everyone knows you're fast and sly. The best thief around."

Sophia drew a weary sigh as she crossed the street with Ginny's arm in hers. "Not for very much longer."

She led the girl to the bench, a sunny spot directly across from Mrs. Prescott's Bridal Agency. Ginny sat and grimaced as she shifted, trying to find a position that would ease the pain in her legs.

"I won't be long." Sophia schooled her features in an attempt to look cheerful. "When I'm done, we'll have a fine afternoon making plans, won't we?"

Ginny shrugged, keeping her gaze averted. Sophia bid her a quick goodbye, squared her shoulders and marched across the street. She couldn't take the time to reassure Ginny. The girl didn't believe Sophia would really take her to Texas. There was no way to convince her that she would never leave her behind. Ever since Ginny had arrived at the door of Boston Municipal Orphan and Foundling Ward, a frightened, silent girl of ten, Sophia had taken her under her wing.

The two girls shared everything, and Sophia wouldn't turn her back on Ginny. Not now. Not ever.

Mrs. Prescott greeted her at the door, her face wreathed in smiles, murmuring kind words. A servant girl took Sophia's cloak, wrinkling her nose at the muddy splashes lining the hem. Without her coat, Sophia shivered. Her thin, well-worn dress held little warmth.

A moment later, she stood in Mrs. Prescott's library. A fire burned in the grate, chasing the chill from the air. Sophia admired the beautiful surroundings and let her gaze linger on the bookshelves lining the walls. Sunshine filled the room, making the chandelier glitter in the winter rays. Men seeking mail-ordered brides paid a price to brokers like Mrs. Prescott, a steep price from the looks of things.

"I'm glad you came when you did. I was about to write Mr. Bentley and inform him of your change of heart," Mrs. Prescott said as she swept past Sophia. "Prideful girl."

"I'm not prideful anymore," Sophia said. "I've changed my heart back. I'm eager to marry and start a family."

Sophia prayed her words sounded sincere and would win Mrs. Prescott over.

Mrs. Prescott nodded. "I'm glad. You seemed so reluctant to have your own brood. The good news is that Mr. Bentley isn't interested in a mob of children either. Just one or two."

Sophia blinked, wondering if a man might bother with a wife if he didn't want a family. She waited for Mrs. Prescott to explain.

"Mr. Bentley seems quite taken with your letters. He said he didn't mind a plain girl."

A plain girl? That was a far different answer than she'd expected. A slow burn of embarrassment crawled across her skin. For as long as she could remember, she'd found safety in her drab appearance. It allowed her a certain freedom that pretty girls couldn't enjoy. While there was hardly any denying that she *was* plain, she didn't much like hearing words that confirmed the fact.

"Mr. Bentley would like a wife who can provide an heir, a son, of course. He mentioned something about his family's legacy."

"Legacy?" Mr. Bentley hadn't told her any of this. Sophia kept her smile in place, resisting the urge to roll her eyes. "Are you sure Mr. Bentley isn't a duke of some sort? Does he have a title to pass on?"

Mrs. Prescott shook her head. "You'd better hold your tongue, missy. He's paid me twice my fee and sent extra funds for you to shop for a few things before you set out to Texas."

Sophia bristled, but kept her thoughts to herself. She thought about Ginny sitting outside in the cool autumn afternoon, trembling in her threadbare coat. She pictured the thin soles of Ginny's boots. She imagined how Ginny might finally have something more for dinner than thin gruel and dried crust, and her heart squeezed as she recalled Silas and his band of ruffians and the way they eyed the frail girl.

Although Sophia had come to Mrs. Prescott's that afternoon to discuss the possibility of taking Ginny with her, she realized she might be able to take her along without asking for anyone's approval. The chance to gain freedom and safety for herself and Ginny sparkled and glittered in her mind's eye, even brighter than the chandelier hanging from the ceiling.

Her mind reeled at Mrs. Prescott's words. *He's paid me twice my fee and sent extra funds...*

She'd come seeking permission.

She'd leave praying for forgiveness.

Sophia leaned forward, her heart crashing against her ribs. "How *much* extra?"

Chapter Two

Joshua Bentley

Josh stood at the corral railing and watched his nephew, Caleb, ride the new gelding. At nineteen, Caleb Bentley was little more than a kid, but in the past few years, the boy had shot up a foot or better. He worked as hard as any of Josh's cowboys, probably harder.

Josh admired the boy's skill. "You might be the only one who can ride Stormy."

"Thank you, Uncle Josh."

"'Bout time for you to get your own place and start your horse ranch," Josh said. "I was about your age when I started out on my own."

"I aim to work for my pa a few more years."

"We're lucky to have you around to help tame these rogue ponies."

Josh had lost count of how many horses Caleb had gentled over the years. While Josh was a fair rider, he was tall and had a muscular build. His weight didn't sit well with the skittish horses. They often objected to having him in the saddle. They pitched and rolled.

Caleb, on the other hand, was lanky and far slighter. He had a way with all animals, it seemed, which was why Josh hired him to work many of the new horses. The young man had his family's work ethic too. Caleb was up before dawn and didn't turn in until he'd outworked all the rest of Josh's hired hands. He didn't work for Josh too often since his father and uncles were unwilling to do without his help.

Caleb spoke softly to the dun and eased him into a lope. The horse obeyed the commands without any fuss. Any other cowboy would have been pitched into the dirt. Stormy was as ornery as the day was long, but with Caleb on his back, the horse seemed as docile as a lamb.

"Did your pa tell you I sent off for a mail-order wife, just like Grace and her sisters?"

Caleb kept his concentration fixed on the horse, but his lips quirked. "No, sir. He didn't."

Caleb continued around the rail until the far side. With a small, deft movement, he reined the horse into the center of the corral, switched leads and turned the other direction. Josh shook his head in disbelief. "Now you're just showing off."

Caleb came back to the middle of the ring and stopped the horse dead in his tracks. Plenty of horses would fuss and toss their head at a sudden halt. Stormy stopped square without a hint of sass. Caleb stroked the horse's neck, praised him and dismounted. He took off his hat and wiped his brow with his shirt sleeve.

"I didn't think you'd ever marry, Uncle Josh."

"Didn't intend to. Not after I got jilted."

The boy's eyes widened. "You got jilted?"

Josh smiled at Caleb's look of surprise. "I did. I was too young. So was she. And when I lost a fortune on one of my stepfather's ventures, she decided she didn't care for me anymore. When that happened, I resolved to a bachelor's life."

"What changed your mind?"

"Getting soft in my old age."

Caleb snorted. "You're what? Twenty-eight?"

"That's right. Getting up there."

The boy didn't go along with the joke. Instead, he kept his somber gaze fixed on Josh, studying him. Josh wondered what he saw. Did Caleb's uncanny awareness of animals also give him a keen understanding of people? The boy seemed to have an intelligence beyond his years. Maybe it was because he'd spent his early life amongst a passel of taciturn cowboys, men who spoke little more than the critters they rode and roped.

Josh, on the other hand, spent his childhood on his family's estate in Houston. His mother and stepfather hobnobbed with the moneyed class of Houston, New Orleans and Atlanta. When he was young, his mother hired governesses to tend to him. When he reached the age of ten, his stepfather sent him to military school.

All the while he yearned for the wide-open land of a cattle ranch, just like the land where his father had grown up. Josh had returned to Magnolia as soon as he could. He'd bought the land his father had owned and then some.

Much to his surprise, his thoughts of late had turned to starting his own family. He was proud of his land and the Bentley legacy. Each time he visited his cousins and saw the Bentley men bringing up their sons, he imagined having a son of his own. If the good Lord blessed him with children, he wouldn't send them off to a harsh boarding school. Nor would he hire womenfolk to care for the boy. He'd keep his son by his side and raise him right, to work hard and fear the Lord.

Caleb turned back to the horse to loosen the cinch. "Grace and her sisters changed everything about my life. I like to think you'd find someone as kind as they are."

"I appreciate that, Caleb. If God blesses me with a son, I'd be mighty pleased if he turned out as fine a young man as you."

The notion warmed his heart and his thoughts went to the girl in Boston. Sophia. He wondered why he yearned so deeply for a woman he hardly knew. His breath hitched as he imagined her arriving in Magnolia. A sweet, kind-hearted, meek and gentle woman. He counted the days until she arrived.

Chapter Three

Sophia

Standing barefooted on the tufted stool, Sophia wriggled her toes in the silken fabric. Mrs. Prescott studied Sophia's reflection in the mirror. She pursed her lips, wrinkled her brow and heaved a tragic sigh.

"The dress might be a little *too* becoming," Mrs. Prescott muttered. "He seemed to prefer an ordinary-looking girl. This might be too much."

"It's very bright," Sophia said. "I never wear blue."

Mrs. Prescott nodded, and her eyes lit with understanding. She turned to the shopkeeper. "That's it. Bring us something in gray or brown."

The shopkeeper managed a weary smile. "Yes, ma'am."

Mrs. Prescott tapped her chin. "Normally, I try to dress my girls to show off their beauty, but Mr. Bentley wants a sturdy girl. He made that clear."

"I'm quite sturdy, I assure you." Part of Sophia wanted to boast how she'd defended one of the younger children against a street thug just that morning. The boy had tried to bully the child out of the penny he'd earned helping sell newspapers. Sophia heard the ensuing commotion out on the street and chased the ruffian. The scoundrel fled in terror the moment he saw her. It might have helped matters that she wielded a garden spade.

Mrs. Prescott made a face. “You might be sturdy if you got a little meat on your bones. Be sure to eat well on the train. Your husband-to-be sent enough money for you to travel in comfort, first-class all the way. I’m most impressed with his generosity.”

“Yes, ma’am.” Sophia smiled sweetly, despite her every intention to swap the first-class ticket for two third-class tickets.

Never had she stepped foot inside such a fancy shop. Dress forms filled the shop’s entry and windows displaying a variety of garments. The more expensive frocks, heavy woolen dresses with elaborate bustles, were precisely what she didn’t want. What did ladies wear in Texas? She couldn’t imagine.

Fortunately, Mrs. Prescott had chosen simpler, more practical dresses, but the color hadn’t been right. Sophia didn’t want to attract attention to herself. She was used to slipping through crowds without drawing anyone’s eye and preferred things that way.

The shopkeeper returned with more dresses. The first was the color of a gray, dreary Boston sky. Perfect. But when Sophia tried it on, she found that the bodice drew tightly across her chest, revealing the curves she always concealed. As she stepped out of the changing room, both the shopkeeper and Mrs. Prescott widened their eyes.

“The color is drab, but the fit is perfect,” the shopkeeper murmured. “What a lovely bride.”

“It won’t do at all,” Mrs. Prescott insisted.

The shopkeeper recoiled. “The price is reduced, and it shows off her pretty blue eyes and raven hair.”

Mrs. Prescott waved her off. “Try on the other, Sophia.”

With a wave of relief, Sophia hurried back to the changing room, yanked off the gray dress and pulled on the brown dress. Unlike the gray dress, the brown one hung more loosely, hiding her curves, thank goodness. When she returned to the salon, Mrs. Prescott smiled with approval.

"Ah, the polonaise. It accentuates your narrow waist. It's flattering but sensible. When you meet your husband-to-be, you should unpin your hair," the shopkeeper suggested. "For a little flare."

Mrs. Prescott knit her brow. "Not at first. Not if you want him to honor the marriage contract. He doesn't seem to want a beauty."

Sophia drew a sharp breath and fisted her hands. "He'd better honor the contract."

Both women stared in wordless surprise. Sophia bit her lip, battling the wave of anger that came over her. Surviving in a crowded orphanage or on the dangerous streets of Boston meant she always had to be ready to defend herself. Things were different now. She would soon be a man's wife. For the present, she needed to keep in mind that she was in the company of gentlewomen, not street thugs.

She coaxed her lips into a ladylike smile. "What I mean is that if he doesn't, I'll simply have to charm him and convince him that I'd be a suitable wife."

Mrs. Prescott gave a nervous laugh as her hands fluttered in the air. "Remember, dear. I have a reputation to uphold."

"Of course," Sophia said in a soothing tone, the one she usually reserved for the babies in the orphanage nursery. She summoned her most innocent expression, the one that always worked with members of the highfalutin sorts. She spoke softly with a tremulous voice. "And if that doesn't work, I'll just resort to tears."

She could hardly recall the last time she cried. She was not a girl prone to weeping, generally speaking, but she could see how the skill of summoning tears might come in handy in managing a husband.

"That's the spirit!" Mrs. Prescott exclaimed.

The shopkeeper and Mrs. Prescott beamed and laughed with relief.

"That's right, dear," Mrs. Prescott added. "You *are* going to make me proud, aren't you?"

"Of course," Sophia said, and promptly bit her lip to keep from saying another word.

Chapter Four

Josh

Every time Josh returned to Houston to visit his mother and stepfather, he wondered how his life might have been if he'd known his father. Some memories of his father lingered in the corners of his mind. There were only a few, sadly. Never enough to suit him. He recalled walking through the wind-swept pastures of the Bentley lands. He'd been only three or so. His father had lifted him to his shoulders to allow Josh a glimpse of the new calf at the far reaches of the field.

It was hard not to compare the misty recollections with the harsh reality of his present-day family.

He tried to ignore his stepfather as the man vented his frustrations regarding yet another business partnership gone sour. His mother sat across from Josh, looking bored. They'd just finished dinner and sat in the dining room of his parents' home, a sprawling Greek revival on the corner of two of Houston's most fashionable streets.

Josh would have liked to tell his stepfather to forget about working with a business partner. His words would have fallen on deaf ears. Nobody told Niles Addington what to do, least of all a wet-behind-the-ears stepson. Instead, Josh suffered in silence as the man hurled angry words and drained glass after glass of scotch. Before long, the man bid them a slurred good night and staggered off to his bedroom.

"Good riddance," his mother said.

Josh refrained from agreeing. "It's nice to have a moment alone, Mother. You're looking well."

She smiled and patted her hair. "Niles and I enjoyed a month at Saratoga Springs. We just got back last Saturday. I think the trip did wonders for my complexion, not to mention my nerves. Niles spent all his time at the horse track, thank goodness, which is probably why I enjoyed myself so much."

"The well-deserved rest did you a world of good," Josh said, hoping his words didn't come across as ironic.

"I saw Bunny Huntington there, darling. You might recall they go every summer. You're lucky the wedding was called off. She looked dreadful. I mistook her for one of the housekeeping staff in the hallway, and accidentally asked her to bring fresh linens. She acted quite offended."

Josh kept from chuckling, but just barely. His mother never made mistakes. He was certain she'd planned to insult Bunny ever since the girl had jilted him years ago. His mother was flighty and busied herself with what he considered foolish pursuits, but she was devoted to him. Always.

"I'm sure that was purely unintended."

His mother gave a throaty laugh. "Of course." She regarded him with an appraising look. "How long will you stay in Houston? Perhaps I can arrange a dinner."

Josh grimaced. This again. "No, Mother. I'm not interested."

"I know so many ladies who would give their eyeteeth to marry their daughters off to you. All my friends talk about what a fine-looking young man you are. Even though you're just a farmer, you're a *very* handsome farmer."

"I'm a rancher."

His mother waved a dismissive hand. "The well-bred society ladies won't hold that against you, not with the fortune you're bound to inherit. Your wife can have a home here amongst civilized folk, while you chase after your cows in the sticks."

Josh drummed his fingers on the table, unaware of what he did until his mother looked askance at his callused hands. She wrinkled her nose. He stopped at once, curling his fingers into a loose fist while he considered his words.

"I've sent off for a bride," he said quietly.

"Finally!" His mother's lips curved into a smile. "Do you mean Felicia Van Hughes from St. Charles?"

Josh groaned. His mother had a special fondness for Felicia, probably because her father owned a shipping company. "No, she's from Boston."

The sound that came from his mother's lips was an excited sort of squeak, one he'd never heard before. She leaned forward, her eyes glittering. "Tell me it's Dorothea Ascot!"

Josh shook his head. "Her name is Sophia."

His mother blinked. Her lip curled. "She sounds foreign. If I didn't know better, I'd think her name was..." Her words trailed off. She took a sip of sherry before continuing in a choked voice. "*Italian*."

"She was raised in the Boston Municipal Orphan and Foundling Ward almost from birth. She's half Italian, half Irish. Her last name is McSweeney."

His mother sank against the back of her chair, her face ashen. After a moment, she closed her eyes, set her hand on her chest and drew a deep breath. When she opened her eyes, she spoke in a quiet but matter-of-fact tone. "You're angry with me, aren't you? You're livid because I didn't invite you to Saratoga Springs and you've come up with this wild, fanciful story to punish me. I meant to invite you. I truly did, but you and Niles would have squabbled all the way and what's the good of repairing my tattered nerves when I'd just end up cooped up on a train with you two men only to suffer through endless bickering? Hmm?"

"Sophia is a mail-ordered bride."

She arched a brow. "What's a mail-ordered bride?"

Josh sighed. This was a game his mother liked to play. If the conversation concerned a common subject, something that would be of interest to ordinary people, she pretended to be too well-bred to have heard of it. Grits, for example. A perfectly decent, delicious and hearty breakfast food, but one Eleanor Addington, Ellie, pretended didn't exist.

If the subject were more rarefied, Cognac, for instance, she'd act as though he were a bumbling oaf, no better than a peasant, for not knowing where the best Cognac came from. The fact that he didn't indulge in spirits hardly mattered.

Josh spoke. "I wrote to a bridal broker, seeking a bride. Mrs. Prescott selected Sophia for me."

His mother's face flushed. "You let a stranger pick out your wife? When you won't let your poor, long-suffering mother suggest a simple dinner party with a suitable, well-connected girl?"

"None of those girls want a life on a ranch."

His mother glared at him. "Of course, they don't. When I married your father, I just pretended to like horses and..." She waved her hand in the air. "And trees. I had no intention of living in a shack."

A shack? His father had offered to build his mother a fine home, but she'd turned her nose up at his efforts, forcing him to choose between his birthright and her. In the end, it hadn't mattered much. His father didn't live more than a few years after they'd married. When he'd died, the Bentley property was promptly sold.

Josh tamped down his bitterness.

"I have no intention of living in a *shack* either. That's why I built a limestone, two-story home with a wraparound porch with a view that would take your breath away." He shrugged. "I've furnished it with an eye to elegance and service. You might even approve, if you ever care to visit."

His mother rubbed her forehead. "Don't hold your breath, darling."

"Maybe you'll come when Sophia and I have a child."

"Oh, Joshua." A whimper fell from his mother's lips, followed by a shudder. "You're going to have children with the Italian-Irish orphan girl. I can't stand it. They'll be odd, backwards little things who reek of garlic and potatoes."

Josh let his mind wander to thoughts of Sophia. Would they be blessed with a child? He'd prayed for a wife and family for so long, he hardly dared to hope. Mrs. Prescott described Sophia as gentle, soft-spoken and biddable. He imagined coming home in the evenings, not to an empty house, but to a house lit by lamplight, and a smiling wife who would greet him with a warm embrace, perhaps a kiss.

He smiled at the heartwarming thoughts, but his mother's scowl yanked him from his reverie.

"You want to raise children out there in wilds?" she asked incredulously.

"I do want children. God willing, I'd like a son to carry on my name and that of my father. When I look at my land, I think about passing it on to a child. I think about a family legacy. And I want a helpmate."

Her frown deepened. "The correct word is *helpmeet*, Joshua. Heavens, the fortune I spent on your schooling."

"I'm sorry, Mother. I want a *helpmeet.*" He smiled inwardly. His announcement had to be a bitter pill for her. She'd always hoped that he would advance the family in the Houston social calendar. A well-connected wife, a lavish wedding, grandchildren she would likely ignore. If he married well, she'd reap untold benefits.

But he didn't need a society wife. He needed much more.

She kept her gaze fixed on him for a long moment. Finally, she let out a trembling sigh. "I've never been able to talk you out of anything. You've always wanted to return to your roots."

Josh set his hand over hers and gave a small squeeze. "I hope you'll come visit."

"Pfft," she scoffed. "I'll come to your dusty ranch to meet your shabby mail-order bride. If only to look you in the eye and say that I told you so."

Chapter Five

Sophia

All her life, Sophia prided herself on her keen judgment and discernment. No matter where she was, whether it be walking on the streets of Boston, or working inside the orphanage walls, she kept a wary eye on her surroundings. Pretending to be blind, therefore, was no easy task. She'd briefly considered having Ginny play the role of blind girl, but Ginny had no ability, whatsoever, to deceive.

They stood on the platform, waiting for the four o'clock train, huddled against the cold drizzle.

Sophia clung to Ginny's arm and spoke to the stationmaster in a trembling voice. "I don't know what to do. I tried to exchange my first-class ticket for two third-class tickets, but third-class is full, they tell me."

The stationmaster had the most curious, bushy eyebrows that seemed to go up and down with each word Sophia uttered. It was a trial not to stare at them. She had to remind herself to gaze, unfocused at some vague spot on his lapel.

"Your sleeper car is for one occupant, miss," he said. "You'll have a chaise, but it's not for sleeping."

"Neither of us is terribly tall. I'm certain we could make do."

The man's brows danced as he considered the predicament. At one point, the man's eyes moved to Ginny, and Sophia couldn't help but stare at his wondrous brows. Luckily, she caught herself and moved her eyes back down to his lapels.

The man had to have noticed that Ginny walked with a limp. He pressed his lips together as if he couldn't decide which of the two girls inspired more of his sympathy.

"We've never been apart," Ginny offered.

"This is most irregular," the man insisted.

Sophia's throat tightened. Everything depended on Ginny coming with her. Otherwise, what was the point? Mrs. Prescott had given her the money Mr. Bentley had sent, but it wouldn't do her any good if there were no tickets to purchase.

Without any other choice, she'd have to employ more of her skills of deception. "Oh, sister, what *ever* will we do?" She cried, making certain to address her words to a loose, navy blue thread on the man's lapel. "This is worse than the accident that lamed you when you were just a child."

She wasn't entirely happy with her delivery. Perhaps mentioning the accident was too much. And her tone had been overly tragic. Ginny sniffled, softly at first and then louder. In the not too-far distance, the train whistle sounded, a plaintive wail caught on the wind. Ginny's crying picked up steam with the approach of the train.

"Don't cry, young lady," the man blurted. "I can't stand a girl's tears."

Ginny wept. Sophia marveled at the girl's theatrics and reconsidered her opinion of Ginny's acting abilities. The ground shook as the train rolled into the station. Sophia resisted the urge to lift her gaze to the approaching engine.

The stationmaster snatched the ticket from Sophia's hand and scribbled on it. "I'm allowing you two young ladies to take the cabin. It wouldn't do for you to sit in third class anyway."

"Thank you, sir," Sophia said with genuine gratitude.

"You two girls remind me of my granddaughters," he grumbled. "I'm quite fond of the pesky girls. I'd hate for them to sit amongst some of the rough folk in third class."

A wave of emotion swept over Sophia making her eyes prickle. She couldn't recall the last time she'd cried real tears, but this man seemed to emanate a heartfelt concern for her and Ginny. The notion warmed her heart. After a lifetime of living amongst the cold and heartless citizens of Boston, her and Ginny's final send-off came from a gruff, but kindly, stationmaster.

The train rumbled into the station and screeched to a stop, the couplings clanging between the cars. Steam billowed from the engine, hissing and spitting. The stationmaster waved a porter over to help with their trunks. Ginny guided her to the train where Sophia made a show of feeling her way along the stair's railing. The porter showed them to their room.

When he'd brought the last of their trunks, Sophia gave him a coin and thanked him.

"First time on a train, miss?"

Sophia set aside her blind charade since the stationmaster had returned to the ticket offices. She stood in the middle of the dormitory and gaped at the luxurious surroundings. "It's the first time for both of us. I've never seen anything so fine."

"Nor have I," said Ginny, running her fingers along the polished wood grain of a chair.

Sophia gestured to the coin, or rather to the young man's clasped hand. "Is that enough? I've never given anyone a tip before."

"Yes, miss. It's more than I usually get. Besides, it was just one small trunk. Thank you." He tipped his hat, smiled and left the compartment.

Ginny grinned at Sophia. "Can you believe our good fortune?"

Sophia went to the window and stood by Ginny, watching the throngs of people bustling throughout the station. Another train arrived on the far track. Passengers disembarked. Some met friends or family on the platform. Sophia watched as people hugged and kissed and welcomed their loved ones.

A pang of sadness squeezed her heart. What would it be like to come home after a long journey and be swept into someone's arms? She could hardly imagine but felt a flicker of envy for the arriving passengers. For the second time that day, her eyes prickled with threatening tears. She gritted her teeth, chiding herself for her foolish sentiments.

She prided herself on her pragmatic outlook. She'd never been one to imagine impossible things or yearn for affection. She was a fixer. A doer. Not a dreamer.

The train whistle rang across the platform. A moment later the train car lurched. Both girls swayed on their feet and shared a wide-eyed look of wonder. They were on their way. The train picked up speed. Another whistle blasted. The station with its crowds slipped from view. They watched in silence as sights of Boston came and went.

For some time, they merely stood at the window and watched. A knock at the door startled them both. A woman's voice came from the door. "Are you the naughty young lady pretending to be blind?"

The woman sounded elderly, her tone suggesting bemusement.

Sophia grinned at Ginny. "I suppose that would be me."

She bit her lip to keep from giggling. What on earth could this be about? Ginny covered her mouth with her hand to silence her laughter.

"Well then, I *suppose* my sister and I would like to invite you and the other little girl to tea."

Chapter Six

Josh

On his last day visiting his mother, Josh came downstairs and heard her talking to someone in the dining room.

"I had such dreams for my son. You know, his grandfather went to West Point?"

"My, isn't that impressive?" a young woman answered.

Josh growled softly as he made his way to the dining room.

"Joshua," his mother exclaimed. "How lovely to see you this morning. I see you've worn your farmer attire. I suppose that means you'll be going home?"

He bent to kiss her cheek and gave a respectful nod to the young lady sitting across the table. "That's right, mother. I believe I told you yesterday. Twice."

"Oh, pooh. I'd hoped to persuade you to stay and take Miss Culver for a turn in the park."

Josh frowned at the young lady. "Fiona Culver?"

Fiona beamed at him. "You remember me, you scamp!"

"Who could forget?"

The young woman's smile faltered.

"What does that mean?" his mother demanded.

"Nothing at all." Josh sat on the other side of his mother and poured himself a cup of coffee. "Just that I remember Fiona from my youth. Her brother, Stephen, and I were friends."

Fiona gave a nervous laugh. "That's right. I'd forgotten."

Josh smiled pleasantly, refraining from any mention of Fiona's overly friendly ways with some of the young men in his circle. Fiona was a well-known flirt, at best. By the time she was twenty, she'd broken several of his friends' hearts, and ended countless engagements.

Sitting across the table, she gave him a coy look. Her dress, a crimson, silken ordeal, clung to her curves, the neckline plunging to reveal that she was no longer just a coquettish girl. Fiona had dressed for business.

"Why, Fiona," his stepfather's voice boomed from the doorway. "If I'd known we had such lovely company, I'd have come to breakfast earlier!"

Niles circled the table, went to Fiona and kissed her hand. "You've certainly grown up, haven't you?"

"Good morning, Niles," Fiona said. "What a surprise to see you."

Josh chuckled as he helped himself to bacon and eggs. "He lives here, you know."

His mother kicked him under the table.

"I know that," Fiona giggled. "Silly."

"So why do you say you're surprised to see my husband?" his mother asked, her tone somewhat chillier than a moment before.

Fiona, never the brightest girl, did manage to pick up on the shift in mood. She blinked and swung her wide-eyed gaze first to Niles, then to Eleanor, and back to Niles. "I thought Niles intended to travel to Mexico. That's what Papa told me."

"Really?" his mother asked drily. "I hadn't heard. How soon are you leaving, darling?"

Niles shook his head, waved his hand and slurped his coffee. The sound always made his mother wince. Even Fiona looked somewhat taken aback by the uncouth noise of his stepfather drinking coffee.

"Not till next week. I'm visiting a silver mine in Guanajuato."

"Oh, dear." His mother lifted her teacup, concealing a smile as she sipped her tea. "That sounds so far away."

Fiona bobbed her head. "And dangerous."

His mother clicked her tongue. "That's right. Far and dangerous." She turned to Josh with a smile, one that didn't quite reach her eyes. "Isn't Fiona a clever girl?"

Fiona's laugh filled the dining room. Josh startled at the noise coming from her mouth. Even his mother stared in horror. Fiona's laugh sounded like a chair scraping across a gritty floor.

His mother sipped her tea. "We'll have to work on that," she murmured under her breath.

While Fiona turned to Niles and batted her lashes, Josh made a show of wiping his mouth with his linen napkin, muttering so only his mother could hear. "Don't bother."

Chapter Seven

Sophia

The dining car, with its mahogany paneling and heavy velvet drapes, was even more elegant than her and Ginny's sleeping car. Two waiters tended to the occupants, gliding up and down the aisle, serving high tea. Sophia sat stiffly, fighting a flush of embarrassment. Ginny, oblivious to her acute discomfort, stared at the tray of petit fours as if she hadn't eaten in a week.

The elderly lady who had introduced herself as Gertrude, or Gertie, poured tea and handed her a cup. "Ooh, Mabel and I spied you on the platform. We wondered why you looked so distressed, so we lowered the window to eavesdrop."

Mabel leaned forward, her eyes sparkling. "I just knew you weren't really blind."

Sophia glanced around nervously, but none of the other passengers appeared to notice. She sipped her tea, coaxing the warm liquid down her tight throat. "I tried to exchange the tickets. The agent said I couldn't, so we didn't have much choice. We had to get on the train or else forfeit our place."

"Good thinking," Gertie said. "My sister and I admire a resourceful girl, don't we, Mabel?"

"We do, indeed. Beauty fades, but a good mind improves with time." Mabel tapped her brow for emphasis.

"Tut, tut. Sophia is both pretty and intelligent."

Ginny laughed softly. "That's what I always tell her. She doesn't believe me though."

Gertie served each of them some of the fancy little sandwiches. "Where are you two girls off to?"

"To Texas. I'm to marry a gentleman in Magnolia." Sophia watched, in dismay, as Ginny wolfed down a sandwich. Before she'd even finished chewing, she snatched the last raspberry scone. Sophia gave a subtle shake of her head. Ginny frowned in response but ignored the silent reprimand. Sophia marveled at Ginny's bold manner. Where was the shy, retiring girl from Boston Municipal Orphan and Foundling Ward?

Mabel saw the exchange and waved off Sophia's concerns. "We have plenty. If we run out, we'll request more. I like to see a girl with an appetite. Both of you could stand to indulge a little. I'm sure your husband-to-be would agree with me. Men like a girl with soft, round arms and curves. Or so I hear. How did you meet your husband?"

"Through a bridal broker in Boston," Sophia said.

Both women gaped. Gertie sat unmoving, her teacup halfway to her mouth, her eyes as big as plums. Mabel stared, slack-jawed.

Ginny shifted nervously in her seat, smoothing her pale hands over her skirts. "He sounds like a very nice man. After all, he sent Sophia plenty of money for her journey."

Mabel waved the waiter over. "Bring us more of everything, if you please."

The waiter bowed, cleared some of the plates and whisked away the empty scone basket.

"Why wouldn't you marry a young man in Boston?" Gertie demanded.

"I want to move to Texas." Sophia nibbled the edge of her watercress sandwich.

After another moment of stunned silence passed, the two ladies smiled amiably and nodded. "It sounds lovely. Do you know very much about your beau?"

"Not much."

"He requested a plain girl," Ginny offered.

Sophia shook her head. "He said he didn't mind a plain girl."

Mabel looked aghast as she fixed her attention on Sophia. "You're certainly not plain. Why, you remind me of our great-niece, Emily. We're just coming from her wedding."

"Rather we *should* be coming from her wedding," Gertie said. "We arrived in Boston to find she'd eloped."

Sophia drew a sharp breath. She was both grateful for the change in subject and intrigued by the story. People she knew didn't elope. Any time she heard about an elopement, the story was about a girl with some social standing. Clearly, both Mabel and Gertie came from wealth, so it didn't take any stretch of the imagination to picture their granddaughter as a girl of means.

"What happened?" Ginny asked.

"It was the most romantic story you've ever heard," Mabel said. She and her sister giggled girlishly.

A romantic notion was a far cry from Sophia's situation. She traveled to Texas for practical reasons, not romance. She sighed, a wistful feeling coming over her heart. Romantic notions about marriage never entered her mind. They were a luxury for other girls.

Mabel began her story. "Emily's parents wanted her to marry her father's business partner."

Ginny murmured with dismay.

"A horrible man. Old, ill-tempered, twice widowed." Mabel grimaced.

“But very rich,” Gertie added. “Very.”

Mabel went on. “But Emily had always loved Arthur, a boy from her youth. One who had very little money.”

“Fortunately, Emily came into a little of her own money.” Gertie batted her lashes. “From a mysterious relative, you might say.”

“From you two ladies?” Ginny asked.

Gertie widened her eyes and drew a small gasp, feigning surprise. “We don’t know what you’re talking about, do we, Mabel?”

“Not the slightest idea,” Mabel replied.

Despite the heaviness wrapped around her heart, Sophia smiled at the two ladies. Emily, wherever she was now, was fortunate to have such kind women watching out for her. Ginny, caught up in the excitement of the story, listened intently as she took a sip of her tea.

The waiter returned with a tray laden with more sandwiches, sweets and a fresh pot of tea. Gertie heaped food on the plates, serving the girls first and her sister and herself last. Ginny pounced on the lemon tart like a ravenous barbarian. Both Gertie and Mabel chuckled.

“Sometime the course of true love,” Mabel said, a smile playing upon her lips, “needs a little capital.”

Gertie nodded. “Capital that my sister and I were only too happy to provide. It was worth it to see her father so outraged, his dastardly plans upended. After he discovered her note, the scoundrel threatened to burn her trousseau.”

“What’s a trousseau?” Sophia asked.

“It’s just a fancy word for a hope chest,” Mabel said. “Don’t you have one?”

Sophia colored. “No, ma’am. I bought this dress, that’s all.”

Ginny shook her head. "Sophia finally buys a new dress and manages to find the ugliest frock in Boston."

Mabel coughed and sputtered. She sipped her tea and waved off her sister's attempts to pat her back. After a few moments, she recovered. "Ginny, really! Sophia, dear, it's a lovely dress." She coughed again and cleared her throat before going on. "It's a very becoming gown. Sensible, you might say."

Sophia pressed her lips together. Mabel was a terrible liar, but Sophia still appreciated the woman's attempt to say something kind.

Gertie had none of her sister's noble intentions. "If you're trying to look plain, you're doing a fine job. That dress makes you look as dreary as a mud hen."

Mabel gasped. "Gertrude, how could you say such a thing? Maybe her husband-to-be is homely. Why else would he require a plain wife?"

Ginny snickered and snatched a dainty, scallop-edged powdered cookie. Clearly, she was enjoying everything about their tea, from the array of delicacies to the lively conversation. Her sugar-covered lips curved with an impish smile as she took a bite of the cookie.

"He might well be homely, but I'm marrying his heart, not his looks. I'll have to be sure to arrive in Magnolia wearing my mud hen dress," Sophia said matter-of-factly.

Gertie's eyes sparkled with amusement. "We'll have to see about that, won't we, Mabel."

"Indeed." Mabel nodded, a smile playing on her lips as she fixed her gaze on Sophia. "We will."

Chapter Eight

Josh

A visit to his mother and stepfather always left Josh bone-tired. Even though he loved his mother, and respected his stepfather, he was grateful to bid them goodbye and leave the bustling streets of Houston. He yearned for the peace and quiet of the countryside.

By late afternoon, he reached his ranch. He rode along the winding trail and across the rolling hills. In the distance, he glimpsed his home. The house and barnyard were deserted. Only a few household staff would be on hand when he returned home, most of them done for the day.

His cowboys, along with his foreman, Francisco, would be gone for another week or two, riding the back pastures. They searched the fields for unbranded youngsters, known as slicks. While Josh didn't worry too much about rustlers, it never hurt to make sure all the new calves wore his brand, a conjoined J and B. The brand was a source of pride too. Fifty years ago, the storied brand had belonged to Jeremy Bentley, his grandfather.

When Josh bought back his father's land, he found the old JB iron in one of the barns. The brand meant a great deal to him. He had come close to losing his dream of owning a ranch when Niles had lost much of Josh's inheritance in a risky investment. Through hard work and the grace of God, Josh had rebuilt his fortune and now owned his family's property along with a respectable home.

What would Sophia think of his house when she arrived in a few days' time?

He imagined she had lived without much luxury. At first, he'd approved of that aspect of the girl. He imagined it would give her a practical outlook on life. Wealth and privilege wouldn't have had a chance to corrupt her. Mrs. Prescott had written to Sophia's school, requesting her records and sent them along with one of her letters.

A bright and apt pupil...

Learns easily and relishes challenging work...

Would excel in advanced studies...

He hadn't requested a nimble-minded girl but had enjoyed reading about her sharp mind. There was more to the girl than he'd imagined. Amongst the reports were comments about her taking on schoolyard bullies. The notion made him smile. Sophia had some mettle. It would serve her well when she came to Texas. The wild country could be a harsh master, not for the faint of heart.

When he arrived home, he untacked his horse, then fed and watered the animal.

He stepped inside his home, shutting the door behind him. The sound echoed across the hallway and up the stairwell. Pausing, he eyed his home, trying to see the surroundings as Sophia might see the house. The antique furnishings he inherited from his grandparents. They lent an elegance he hoped would please Sophia.

He went upstairs to the room she'd use when she first arrived. Leaning against the doorway, he took in the details of the room, the lacy bedspread, the hand-threaded rug on the floor and the French doors that led to a balcony. A stack of linens sat on the bed, towels and whatnot that he'd ordered embroidered with the initials SB, her married initials.

Sophia had tried to wriggle out of their arrangement, for some reason. By then he'd already ordered the linens and had them personalized just for her. He tugged an envelope from his breast pocket, noting the hitch in his heartrate. The photograph, a grainy daguerreotype, didn't capture her image. Not properly.

"She's sly," the Pinkerton man had grumbled. "Crafty just like all them foundlings."

None of the other photographs were any better. All of them were blurry, or merely showed her narrow shoulders or back. Only this picture, the one he'd carried for the last three months, hinted at what Sophia McSweeney looked like. The image showed her turning, her dark hair arranged in a twist that revealed the graceful curve of her neck.

"She's partial to one of the other orphans, a girl named Virginia, but they call her Ginny. A slight little thing with a limp. The girl looks like a stiff wind might knock her to the ground," the Pinkerton man had written. "The two girls are always together. Mark my words, your sly girl will find a way to bring her to Texas. Word is that whenever the girl needs something, Sophia gets the money by pickpocketing. She's a little thief. Never for her own gain, but for the other children in the orphanage."

At first, the agent's letter had annoyed Josh. Maybe Sophia would be too willful to make a good helpmeet. A day or so later, he admitted, if only to himself, a grudging respect for Sophia. She had grit and intelligence and loyalty, traits he admired in a man or woman.

Closing the door to her room, he crossed the hallway to another bedroom. The room's ceiling angled due to the eaves above, but the late afternoon sunshine filled it with warm light. The Pinkerton man knew his business. When Josh considered that not one, but two, young ladies might arrive on the train, he resolved to make the stowaway as welcome as possible.

He smiled wistfully and drew the door shut.

Chapter Nine

Sophia

On the fifth morning of travel, Sophia woke to a knock at the door. She dressed hurriedly, trying not to disturb Ginny. Despite her efforts, Ginny woke anyway and sat up on the chaise and rubbed her eyes.

"Who is it?" she whispered.

Sophia finished dressing. "I don't know."

She cracked the door to find Gertie and Mabel outside. They grinned at her, each with a mischievous gleam in their eye. Sophia tried to clear her jumbled mind. Why were the two ladies at her door? Had they made plans for breakfast? She couldn't recall, but they'd eaten breakfast, lunch and dinner each day since boarding the train. Perhaps they'd made plans and the details escaped her memory.

"We're departing the train in an hour," Gertie said with more excitement than Sophia thought the comment called for.

"Oh, dear," Sophia said. "I'm so sorry to see you go."

She'd relished the women's company, as had Ginny. The prospect of traveling the rest of the way to Texas without their companionship seemed daunting. Panic squeezed her heart. The sensation surprised her since she prided herself on her courage.

Mabel spoke. "You and Ginny must come to our room. We ordered breakfast for the four of us."

"Of course. Thank you," Sophia said. "We'll be along shortly."

She and Ginny took some time to fix themselves, brushing their hair and getting fully dressed. Sophia caught sight of herself in the looking glass. She paused, studying her reflection, while Ginny finished lacing her boots. Mabel's and Gertie's departure made the prospect of marriage seemed so much closer.

"I never expected I'd really be someone's wife," she murmured.

Ginny crossed the small room, wincing at a pain in her leg. "What did you expect?"

"To be a washerwoman." She gazed at her hands. "A child minder, a cook or whatever was needed at the orphanage."

Ginny rubbed her fingers across Sophia's palm. "Your hands are already softer. You're not a washer woman or any of those things anymore."

"Don't you suppose my homely husband will expect me to mend and wash his ragged clothes?" Her voice sounded hollow as if someone had drained all the life from her words. The worry about what might happen when she reached Texas wore her out, making her feel the most peculiar sort of exhaustion.

"Yes, but that won't be the only thing you'll do. You'll cook and tend your home and keep him company."

"I hope he finds me pretty."

"You are, Sophia. One day I'm going to sew you a dress that isn't the color of a muddy, rushing river."

Sophia smiled sadly. She wondered, her heart quaking, if she might be able to convince Josh Bentley to allow Ginny to remain, even if just for a short while. Or would he rage at her?

Perhaps he would refuse them both, and then what? Would she need to dust off her criminal talents?

"My stomach's growling," Ginny said, nudging her toward the door.

They went to the next car and knocked on Mabel and Gertie's door. The two sisters invited them in, sat them at the table and served them a sumptuous breakfast. Sophia pushed aside all her doubts and fears and tried her best to put on a brave face. The sisters were leaving, and their departure felt like a terrible loss despite having known the women only a short while.

"We insist you write to us," Gertie said. "Kansas City isn't so far that we can't come for a visit."

"Or to whisk you away from your husband, if he's a beast," Mabel added.

"Hush, Mabel. Don't frighten the poor bride."

Sophia let out a soft huff of dismay. She was a bride. It was true. Closing her eyes, she said a quick prayer, asking for strength to follow through with her plan, if only for Ginny's sake.

Mabel set her hand on Sophia's and gave her a warm squeeze. "I mean what I say. We might look harmless, but both of us know how to give a brute a good knock with an umbrella."

"Or what have you," Gertie added.

Ginny grinned at both of them. "That sounds like Sophia. She's not much bigger than me but takes on the worst of them in a pinch. She's not afraid."

Sophia coaxed her lips into a smile. "I am now, a little. I'll meet my husband-to-be in just a few days. What if he doesn't like me?"

Ginny rolled her eyes. “The dress is ghastly. He might run screaming when he sees you.”

Mabel and Gertie nodded. Mabel spoke. “That’s what we thought too.”

Sophia frowned at the three of them. “I should have kept my thoughts to myself.”

“We have something for you, Sophia.” Gertie rose and went to the far side of the sleeper car. She opened a large steamer trunk that sat beneath the window. “Come have a look at your trousseau, dear.”

Sophia drew a sharp breath. She got to her feet and crossed to stand beside Gertie. The trunk was filled, overflowing with dresses and lacy underthings, boots and shoes, hats and scarves.

“W-where did this all come from?” Sophia asked.

“When our granddaughter eloped, she didn’t take anything along. Her father vowed to burn her trousseau, but Mabel and I packed it away secretly before he could get his hands on it. Afterall, we’d given her a great deal of money to buy all these fine things.”

Mabel sniffed. “We paid for everything. It was before we knew the details of the despicable man her father insisted she marry. We did it because we love Emily. The trousseau is ours.”

Gertie nodded. “And now it belongs to you.”

Sophia set her hand over her heart and gaped at the abundance of feminine things spilling from the chest. She’d never had anything new until Mrs. Prescott bought her the dress she now wore. All her life, she’d worn dresses and boots that had belonged to one of the other girls in the orphanage.

“You’re the same size as Emily, or close enough,” Mabel said. She tugged a dress from the trunk, a blue silk frock. The dress had a basque bodice, a pleated skirt and a cambric jabot. "This should fit you. Go on. Try it on."

Sophia took the dress and went to the water closet, feeling as if she were in the midst of a dream. Mabel was right. The dress fit. It showed off her figure without making her feel ashamed of her womanly curves. Even the length was perfect. Clasping her brown dress in her trembling hand, she returned to where the ladies waited.

Ginny made a face and snatched the brown dress from her hands. "Spin around. Show off a little, Sophia."

Sophia turned around, feeling utterly foolish being on display.

"You, my dear, will make a lovely bride," Mabel whispered.

Gertie said nothing, but nodded, her eyes shining.

"Right," Ginny said matter-of-factly. "Much, much better. You're ready for Texas. Almost." With that, she went to the window, jerked the sash and pulled it down. The clatter of the wheels filled the small room. Wind whipped Ginny's hair, tugging swathes free from her braid. With a quick motion, she flung Sophia's brown dress out the window. In an instant, it vanished. Ginny heaved the window shut and turned to face them with a satisfied smile. "*Now*, you're ready for Texas."

Chapter Ten

Josh

While Josh Bentley didn't consider himself the best cowboy on his ranch, he relished the hard work. His favorite time of the day was the quiet just before dawn. He'd begin work before daybreak. At the end of the day, he'd fall into bed feeling sore, tired but satisfied. Working the land fulfilled him unlike anything else.

Before his move to the country, Niles had given him work in the family business, but Josh had disliked it intensely. He spent his days tied to a desk, one that was made of mahogany, but a desk, nonetheless. The work was dull, nothing like laboring with his hands, or working cattle from the back of a horse.

Francisco and the ranch hands regarded him with respect. Not because he always knew how to manage every aspect of ranch work, but because when he didn't know, he asked, or read up on the matter, or otherwise schooled himself.

The hard-won education came at a price. Every morning he began in the pre-dawn darkness. He could have remained in bed and left the tasks to the ranch hands. They would do the work without complaint, but feeding and grooming the horses, repairing and cleaning tack and otherwise preparing for the day meant something to him. The work sustained him. It nourished his soul.

The morning that Sophia was expected to arrive at the Magnolia train station, he left the house to do his usual list of chores. Stars twinkled in the ebony skies. The planet Venus gleamed in the east. Where was she, he wondered. He supposed she traveled somewhere along the lonesome stretch of prairie between Fort Worth and Magnolia. He trudged across the barnyard, gravel crunching beneath his boots. He tried to picture her, sleeping in her berth. Maybe the other girl slept nearby, if she'd come along.

By that afternoon, he'd know much more.

With a grateful heart, he worked in the early morning stillness. The faint gleam of dawn, a rose-colored ribbon on the distant horizon, inspired him to stop his work and give thanks for the ranch, his home and a chance to reclaim his birthright. He added a new sentiment to his prayers.

Watch over my family, including my new family, Sophia. And her friend too.

He fed his horses, working distractedly as he tried to imagine the girls' arrival that afternoon. He had no idea what would come of an extra girl in the house, but he knew he'd do what he could to make her feel at home. Ginny was her name, if he remembered correctly from the Pinkerton man's letter. He'd broached the subject of Ginny with his Bentley cousins and their wives.

At first the three women expressed shock and even a little indignation that Sophia might bring another girl. They'd changed their minds, however, when Josh explained that the girl worked in the orphanage nursery. He'd added that she had been bullied by others in the orphanage. Upon hearing that news, all three agreed it was best that she come along. Their distress over her mistreatment turned to vying with each other to lay claim to a girl who might help with their growing brood.

"It's good of you to take in the other girl," Grace commented. "You're showing your Christian duty."

"That's not how I see it," he'd replied. "Sophia's coming all this way to be my wife. I owe her my gratitude. The girl is the closest thing Sophia has to a sister, just like you three ladies."

Grace nodded. "That's true."

"Sophia and I won't always agree, of course. But for the most part, I'll always want just exactly what she wants."

The women, along with the men, got over their astonishment. He could only imagine what his mother might say to such a notion. Likely she would never find out, since she never visited Magnolia.

After he finished his chores, he worked on the corral gate, repairing the latch. Time passed slowly. He was impatient. Despite his eagerness to set off, he returned to the house and took a light lunch, a sandwich he ate standing by the warmth of the stove.

His cook, Rosalinda, smiled fondly at him. "It will be nice to have a young girl or two in the house. And maybe a child one day, no?" She crossed herself and kissed her fingers. "*Ojala*."

He grinned and took a swallow of coffee. "God willing and the creek don't rise."

"It's a good thing," she said, returning her attention to stirring the pot of chili. "A man needs company."

"What about women?" he teased. "You and Francisco have been married, what? Twenty-five years?"

She muttered a stream of Spanish, lifted her eyes, added a few words in an imploring tone and returned her attention to the fragrant stew.

"I take that as a yes," Josh said.

"Yes." She huffed an exasperated sigh, but her frown faded as a slow smile tugged at her lips. "Twenty-five years."

Josh gestured towards the bubbling stew. "This is the first meal my wife's going to eat in our home? Chili? Are you testing her, Rosalinda?"

She chuckled. "Maybe I should make something fancy, eh?"

He crossed the kitchen, stopping at the door. "Might be better to ease her into your spicy cooking."

"All right," she said with a weary sigh. "I'll make a roast with potatoes."

"Thank you." He went upstairs, washed, shaved and dressed in his Sunday best.

He drove the buckboard into Magnolia, a sense of anticipation growing with each passing mile. His mother, his stepfather and maybe, to some extent, even Rosalinda, thought sending for a mail-order bride was a terrible idea. Even his Bentley cousins, who had sent for mail-order brides themselves, seemed to worry about his plan.

Having lost his father, and then his family's land, gave him a deep determination to forge his own path. For some reason, he felt deep in his heart that Sophia would help him reclaim what he'd lost. He had no reasoning other than what lay in his heart. Perhaps his heart had its own reasons.

When he arrived at the train station, he left the team at the hitching rail and made his way to the platform. A crowd had gathered, rough workmen, miners and cowboys. He was glad the train hadn't yet arrived. Sophia would be one of the only women disembarking. He didn't like the idea of her mixing with this rowdy group of townsfolk.

Soon the train's whistle pierced the cold winter afternoon. A plume of smoke rose in the cloudless sky. The ground shook as the train rounded the bend in the track. Josh pressed forward, moving in the direction of the first-class passenger car.

And then he saw her. Sophia. She stood in the doorway, a small, delicate girl by her side.

With his feet rooted to the spot, he could only watch as she descended the steps. She didn't wear a bonnet. Her dark hair gleamed in the sunshine. Her eyes, light colored, blue, maybe gray, scanned the crowd.

He watched, enraptured. His Sophia was here. He followed her gaze to a shabby-looking cowboy who for some reason waved at her. Joshua could see from her expression that she thought the rumpled older man was him. He growled. No one would ever accuse him of being vain, but it wounded his pride that she looked upon the disheveled rascal, and imagined it was her husband.

Josh pushed his way through the crowd. He watched in astonishment as she extended her hand to the ranch hand. The man wore a tattered and soiled jacket. A hat with a broken brim, and a misbuttoned shirt.

"Joshua Bentley?"

Her voice sent a shiver across Josh. She didn't address him, but he still felt a curious awareness at the sound of her voice.

"Howdy, ma'am," the cowboy muttered, sweeping his grimy hat from his head.

Josh tried to move through the mob of people, his progress hindered. He could only watch as his bride spoke to a stranger, thinking it was him.

"I've always fancied dark hair and blue eyes," the cowboy said.

Sophia's smile faltered. "I'm very pleased to meet you. I believe my trunks will be along in a moment. The porter said he'd bring them at his first chance."

"You sure are a purdy little thing," the man said, slurring slightly. "What's your name, darlin'?"

Sophia's eyes widened. She moved back a few steps, drawing the girl closer.

Joshua called to her, just as the train whistle blew. He tried to reach her, but his path was blocked by two porters carrying a long wooden crate. He ducked under and hurried, trying to close the distance between him and his bride.

"Go on, tell me your name," the cowboy said. "I'm just bein' friendly."

"Sophia," Josh shouted across the crowd.

She turned to face him, a stunned expression on her face. The girl, holding Sophia's arm, sprang to action. She pulled Sophia away from the unkempt cowhand, through the mass of people and stopped before Joshua.

"I'm Ginny," the girl offered, a sunny smile curving her lips. "This is Sophia."

Josh swept his hat from his head and smiled at the girl. "I'm glad you decided to come, Ginny."

Sophia had turned pale. She stared at him, her eyes widened in astonishment. Her dark locks caught the breeze and swirled around her pretty face, the small swathes framing her lovely features. She swallowed hard but said nothing, seemingly too stunned to say a word of greeting.

"It's a good thing," Ginny replied. "If I hadn't, Sophia might have married that fellow back there."

She gestured to the grizzled cowboy who had greeted the girls a moment before. The man peered through the crowd, looking at the girls with a deep frown. He scratched his uneven beard, waved a dismissive hand and wandered off into the throng of people.

"You're not what I expected," Josh said, taking Sophia's hand in his.

When Sophia still didn't reply, Ginny spoke on her behalf.

"Neither are you," Ginny said, almost shouting over the crowd. "We didn't know what to expect. He's handsome, right, Sophia? Not homely at all."

The girl elbowed Sophia in the side.

Josh chuckled. "Sophia can talk, is that right?"

"Oh, sure," Ginny said. "She talks plenty."

A porter appeared in the train's doorway. He stood on the platform, looking here and there, scanning the crowd. Joshua assumed he looked for the girls and lifted his hand to wave, but before he could get the man's attention, Ginny gave a sharp whistle. The porter nodded and brought a small trunk. Two men followed, carrying a larger trunk.

Joshua directed the men to the buckboard. Like Sophia, he felt dazed by their first meeting. He watched the men load the trunks onto the back of the wagon. When the porters were done, they stood about for a long awkward moment, tipping their caps at Sophia and Ginny.

Ginny grinned at him, pulling him from his confusion. "I think they're waiting for a tip, Josh."

Sophia startled and reached for her purse. Joshua's face warmed. He'd tipped porters or bellmen a thousand times before. What on earth had come over him? He dug in his pocket and pulled out a few coins, tipped the young men and sent them on their way.

He cleared his throat and tried to collect his scattered thoughts. "Right. We need to go see the gunsmith."

Ginny and Sophia both stared at him. Even Ginny was too surprised to respond to his comment.

Josh raked his fingers through his hair. "We don't have regular services in Magnolia, but, come to find out, the Magnolia gunsmith is also a pastor."

The train whistled. The conductor yelled, "All aboard." Josh waited for one of the girls to say something, but both simply continued to stare. One of the horses in his team pawed the ground impatiently.

"I thought we'd get married, Sophia. Before I take you to my home. I think it best if we're man and wife if you're living under my roof." He tugged at his collar, wondering why all of a sudden it felt so blasted tight. "If you're willing, that is."

Sophia nodded and spoke, finally. Her voice was soft and feminine and unlike a few moments ago when she spoke to the cowboy on the platform, it sounded a little tentative. Not surprisingly.

"All right," she said, barely breathing the words. And in a little stronger tone she added, "I'm willing."

Chapter Eleven

Sophia

They spoke their vows in the dusty gun shop. The gunsmith seemed impatient to get back to a card game in the back of the shop. The men yelled for him to get a move on and called him a yellow-bellied coward for leaving when he was losing. Sophia could only gape at her surroundings and murmur her part of the vows because it all seemed to be part of a dream.

After their vows, Josh took them to his home. The scenic drive through the countryside kept Sophia awestruck.

"You like it?" Josh asked.

"It's the prettiest thing I've ever seen."

He smiled at her. His approval filled her chest with warmth. She thought back on his words about their marriage and how it was meant to be. For the first time in her life, she wondered if there was such a thing as meant to be. He might think differently about her if he knew about her past transgressions.

A twinge of nervousness came over her, but she tamped it down. She'd tell him one day, she promised herself. In the meantime, she'd need to make certain Ginny didn't breathe a word about the short but shameful chapter in her life. In her mind's eye, she saw Ginny, with very short hair, after she'd sold her beautiful locks to pay Sophia's counselor.

Ginny sat beside her, looking awestruck at the picturesque, sun-dappled lands. Silently, Sophia said a prayer of thanksgiving that Josh hadn't said a word of complaint about Ginny. How, she wondered, had she managed to find such a kind and noble man? He was handsome too. She stole a glimpse of his profile as he drove the team of horses. He met her eye and gave her a bemused smile.

His glance made butterflies flutter inside her, a feeling that was both pleasant and terrible. She forced herself to keep her attention away from Josh for the rest of the trip.

The house was beautiful, far from the dusty hovel she'd envisioned. Made of roughhewn timbers and massive blocks of stone, Josh's home looked as strong as a fortress. And yet it offered a softer touch. Benches and rockers sat on the front porch and gave the home an inviting appeal.

When Josh helped her down, he clasped her waist and held her gaze. His touch stole her breath. She chided herself for her foolishness.

He left them in the foyer, promising to return after he'd unhitched the horses. Ginny and Sophia stood in the entry, both too awed to move.

Sophia swayed, suddenly overcome with a storm of emotions, her world tilting precariously. She reached for the banister of the staircase, but her hands slipped from the gleaming mahogany. She sank against the balustrade, her strength wilting. Ginny crossed the foyer and wrapped a supportive arm around her waist.

"What's wrong, poppet?" she teased. "Ain't never seen a fancy house before? Or was it the kiss your husband gave you when the two of you said your vows?"

A rush of embarrassment bloomed inside Sophia. "I hardly recall the kiss. Or the vows."

"I do. It was lovely," Ginny said. Her tone, no longer teasing, held a note of warmth. "The way Josh looked at you made me think that he doesn't see you as plain. Not at all. I never have either. Your brown dress, on the other hand, is another matter entirely."

"Hush, Ginny," Sophia murmured.

If Sophia hoped for a shred of sympathy from Ginny, she got none. The girl frowned at her and shook her head with clear disapproval.

"Get a hold of yourself, Sophia. You've faced worse than marrying a man who admires you and wants to give you a fine home. Pull yourself together and I'll help you with your trunks. I want to see your room. Josh said it's at the top of the stairs, second door on the left."

"He did?"

Ginny rolled her eyes. "It was probably while you were shaking like a frightened rabbit. If you faint, I'll leave you lying where you fall."

Her taunting words shook Sophia from her daze. "I've never fainted in my life!"

Ginny gave her a slight push. "Good. Don't start now. Let's tend to the trunks. We'll take the fancy one first. The *trousseau.*"

She made a show of acting like a fancy lady and snickered at her own silliness. They each grabbed a handle on the steamer trunk and began the arduous trip up the stairs. The stairs were twice the number of steps of any other staircase, but Sophia didn't dare complain. Not if Ginny didn't. The girl toiled tirelessly step by step, with as much effort as Sophia, despite her old injuries.

They paused three quarters of the way up to catch their breath. "Don't hurt yourself," Sophia muttered.

“Oh, hush,” Ginny fussed. “We’re almost there.”

“I should give you some of these dresses. We could take them in and raise the hem.”

“No need. I’ll manage with what I brought.”

They lugged the immense trunk up the rest of the steps and managed to haul it to the room, only dropping it twice. Fortunately, the trunk didn’t harm the wooden floor. They pulled it into a corner of the bedroom and set it down. Their task carried out, both girls took in the details of the bedroom.

Sophia had never had a room all to herself. The bed, iron-framed and covered with a brightly colored quilt, looked like it could sleep three people. She went to the window, brushed the delicate, lace curtains aside and searched the barnyard for Joshua. Aside from a few dogs and a cat perched on a fencepost, the yard was deserted. When they’d arrived, an older man, a cowboy by the name of Jess, had helped unload the trunks and left with Josh to tend to the horses, but there wasn’t a sign of either of them now.

The slam of the downstairs door made Sophia jump. Heavy footsteps followed and a moment later, Josh appeared in the doorway of her bedroom. The sight of him in the doorway reminded her of his height and brawn. His build had been hewn from the hard work he did each day. A shiver of awareness ran across her skin as she recalled the way he’d cupped her shoulders and brushed a kiss across her lips.

“Who brought up the trunk?” His gruff tone made his displeasure clear.

His tone took her by surprise. He’d been all sweet words and glances when she sat next to him on the buckboard. Now he looked chagrined. “Ginny and I brought it up,” Sophia said. “Should we not have done that?”

To her surprise, his frown deepened. "I'd asked Jess to come over when he was done and help with your baggage."

"We're used to fending for ourselves," Sophia said.

Josh folded his arms across his chest. "Not anymore."

Ginny chuckled. "Aw, that's sweet."

"It's not *sweet*." Josh turned his gaze to the girl. "Virginia."

"Hate that name," Ginny muttered.

"How did you know Ginny was coming?" Sophia asked, unable to contain her curiosity. She'd expected him to be indignant about an extra girl coming. Instead, he was annoyed that they'd carried up their own trunk. "When we arrived, you seemed as though you expected her."

Ginny gave a huff of surprise. "I thought you told him!"

Sophia ignored the girl, keeping her gaze fixed on Joshua. He smirked, saying nothing. Worry twisted inside her chest. "It's not fair, is it? You know about things about me, yet I know very little about you."

He shrugged. "When you told Mrs. Prescott that you didn't want to come to Texas to marry me, I hired a Pinkerton man."

"You spied on me?" Sophia asked.

"I thought he knew I was coming," Ginny said, panic edging her voice.

"I did spy on you," Josh said, addressing Sophia. "I'd already grown fond of you, or fond of what Mrs. Prescott told me. I wanted to be certain you were safe and sound and that no one threatened you."

Ginny snorted. "No one threatens Sophia. Not if they like having a full set of teeth."

Ginny's words fanned the flames of Sophia's indignation. "Hush, Ginny. Hold your tongue."

Josh seemed to think Ginny's words were amusing. He leaned against the doorway and smiled as if he were having a fine time at Sophia's expense. But there was nothing funny about the situation. If the Pinkerton man had done his job, Josh would know far more about her past than she wanted him to know.

Ginny seemed to think *she* was the offended party. She sniffed and turned away, crossing to the window. Her limp was more pronounced as it was whenever she forgot to pay attention to her uneven gait. "I apologize, Josh. I'm sorry to impose on your hospitality."

Sophia shook her head at Ginny's response. The girl liked to put on airs when she was put out. When she was truly angry, she could swear like the worst of them. Still, something about Ginny's distress pulled at Sophia's heart as it always did. Standing by the window, the last rays of dusk lighting her girlish features, Ginny looked small and vulnerable.

"Ginny," Josh said quietly. "I've been blessed. I have more than I need. I am mighty glad you've come to Texas. I knew you and Sophia are like sisters. You will have a place in my home as long as you like."

"Thank you," Ginny said, turning to face him.

"You're just a child, after all," he said.

"I'm fifteen," she said, her brow knit.

Josh set his hand over his heart. "I didn't realize you were so aged. When you two ladies are ready, please come downstairs so that we can have dinner."

When he was gone, his footsteps fading downstairs, Ginny turned to her. "Well, he didn't throw us out on our ear."

Sophia turned away to hide her distress. "Not yet."

Chapter Twelve

Josh

Josh never imagined a horse would get the better of Caleb Bentley. The young man lay in the dirt, groaning. The bay gelding that had just bucked him off trotted around the corral, snorting, his tail in the air.

With a sharp whistle, Josh called the horse. The animal crossed the corral at once, but pranced around, just out of reach, still full of trouble and tricks. Josh edged closer, talking in a low, soothing tone until he could grasp the reins. He waited for the young cowboy to recover from his humiliation.

Caleb sat up, rubbed the back of his neck and groaned. "Can't remember the last time I got pitched off a horse."

"Feeling all right?" Josh asked.

Sophia swept the porch, and Ginny sat in a rocker, reading a book. They both stopped what they were doing and hurried over. This was their first morning on the ranch, and probably the first time they'd seen someone get tossed by a frisky mustang.

"My gosh," Ginny exclaimed. "That must have hurt!"

Sophia nodded. "Are you injured?"

Caleb shook his head, got to his feet and brushed himself off. Josh noted the way the boy's face reddened. He couldn't help feeling a pang of sympathy for Caleb, especially after the boy had asked at least a dozen questions about Ginny. Word about an extra girl from Boston had traveled fast.

"No, ma'am," Caleb muttered. "I'm fine. Just got a little careless, that's all."

Careless? Josh tried not to scoff. The boy had been distracted by Ginny. He'd stolen furtive glances at the girl while she read and hadn't paid attention to his work. Josh shook his head and tried to keep from chuckling at the mishap.

"Don't feel badly," Ginny suggested. "I'm sure everyone falls off at first."

"Thanks a lot," Caleb said from between gritted teeth.

Josh turned away to hide his grin. He made a show of checking the cinch, keeping his back to Caleb to avoid hurting his pride any further. Josh was pleased that Sophia had ventured out to the corral.

He glanced over his shoulder to steal a quick glimpse at his bride. She wore a dark blue dress. Her thick hair was swept into an elegant twist. He couldn't help a glimmer of pride. Sophia was as pretty as any of the society girls in Houston. Unlike them, she had a presence about her. Yesterday she'd been shocked that he had a cook, and even more astonished when Rosalinda shooed her out of the kitchen, refusing to let her wash up after dinner.

This morning, she'd insisted on taking some part of tending to the house. She talked Rosalinda into giving her a broom so she could sweep the leaves off the porch. Standing by the railing, she kept her attention fixed on Caleb, her lips pursed, and brow knit with worry. She must not have realized that it took a lot more than a spill from an ornery horse to hurt a cowboy.

Caleb came to his side and took the reins from him. He swung into the saddle. Josh could see the grim determination in his eyes.

"Don't let him hurt you," Ginny called. She made a fist and hit the railing with her small, clenched hand. "I've read books about cowboys. They say you've got to show him who's boss."

Caleb pulled the horse to a halt and backed it several paces. "I got this. Thank you."

Sophia turned to Josh. "Rosalinda wanted to know if you'd come for lunch."

"Tell her I'll be there at noon."

With a nod and one final, fretful look at Caleb, she turned and began back to the house. Ginny followed, keeping up despite her limp.

"Wonder what's wrong with her leg?" Caleb asked.

"She got injured. Hurt it when she was a kid and it didn't mend right." Josh winced thinking about Ginny suffering as a child. He'd liked the girl right from the start. She and Sophia had a sweet, sisterly friendship, one minute fussing at each other, the next laughing together. Josh appreciated the girl's sunny disposition. Even Rosalinda remarked that the girl was a delight, making a fuss over her that morning at breakfast.

"When did she tell you that? Didn't she just get here yesterday?"

"I heard about what happened before she got here."

Josh didn't feel like divulging the details of his Pinkerton man. Now that he had Sophia here in Texas, the notion struck him as unseemly. He'd seen the pain and surprise in her eyes when he told her he hired the detective. Josh hired the man out of concern for Sophia, but she hadn't seen it that way.

Caleb watched Ginny as she and Sophia returned to the house. Josh felt a wave of protectiveness come over him. Ginny might be fifteen, but she was slight, giving the impression of being far younger than her years. While Josh didn't really know her well, or Sophia for that matter, he had a strong desire to shield her from admiring looks. At least for a short while, the girl should be allowed to just be a girl. Adult circumstances and responsibilities would come soon enough.

"Whatever you're thinking about, you might as well just put it out of your head," Josh said gruffly.

Caleb startled. His face reddened. "Yes, sir. I just think she's..."

His words faded. He looked sheepish as he pressed his lips together and shook his head.

"You're a mite young too," Josh added. "No need getting romantic notions in your head."

"No, sir."

Caleb turned the horse toward the rail and resumed his work. Josh remained where he stood, trying to reconcile the desire to protect both Sophia and Ginny from any threat. Not that Caleb Bentley presented much of a danger to any woman, but Josh could imagine how other young bucks around Magnolia might grow interested in Ginny over time.

His attention drifted back to the porch. Sophia had set aside her broom and sat beside Ginny. If he felt glimmers of protectiveness over Ginny, it hardly compared to the emotions he felt for Sophia. Since the moment he'd laid eyes on Sophia, her welfare and happiness had consumed his thoughts. He wanted to do everything he could to keep her safe and bring a smile to her lips.

Ginny worked on something she held in her hands. It looked like she was working on a sock, darning it, of all things. He wanted to storm back to the house, pull it from her hands and explain that she'd never have to darn another sock. Not under his roof. He resisted the urge, however, in an attempt not to start the day with a disagreement, like the one they'd had yesterday over the trunk. Sophia didn't want him to fuss over her. She tried to keep him at an arm's length. While Ginny was bright and cheerful, Sophia was quiet and reserved. He needed to find a way to reach his bride's guarded heart.

Chapter Thirteen

Sophia

Sophia and Ginny had been there three days when the cowboys returned from the pastures with a herd of yearlings. Their arrival stirred up a great deal of excitement and commotion. Ginny and Sophia went down to the barnyard that afternoon to watch the men, about a dozen or so, ride in. Rosalinda, the cook, tagged along, caught up in the excitement and eager to see her husband.

In addition to the cattle, the men drove a herd of horses. The men put them into a fenced field on the far side of the barnyard. After that, the men dismounted, unsaddled their horses and let them loose along with the others. The sight of the horses grazing belly-deep in the sea of grass stole Sophia's breath.

"They're beautiful," she said. "Nothing like the horses in Boston."

"They're mustangs," Rosalinda said. "Here in Texas we have large herds that run free."

"Were the horses that didn't have a rider part of the wild herds?" Ginny asked.

"No." Rosalinda shook her head. "Each morning, a cowboy takes a horse from the group. Sometimes he changes horses in the afternoon, because the animals get tired. The group of spare horses is called a remuda."

Each day, Sophia realized there was so much to learn about life on a Texas ranch. She yearned to know more, but Josh didn't seem to want her company or her help. Twice she'd offered to help him with some chore. Both times he'd rejected her offer.

One of the cowboys swept his hat from his head, called Rosalinda's name as he waved from the corral. Rosalinda chuckled and waved back. "That's Francisco, my husband. I want to make him his favorite pie. Would you like to help me pick nuts from the orchard?"

Both Sophia and Ginny were more than happy to go with Rosalinda. Sophia was embarrassed to admit she'd never seen an orchard before. For as long as she could remember, she'd lived amongst the crowded, poor Boston tenements, far from parks and the smallest glimpse of nature. Texas was so different. The land brimmed with trees and grasses and wide-open sky.

Rosalinda brought a basket. On the way to the orchard, they stopped by the henhouse and gathered eggs. Both Ginny and Sophia laughed at the way the chickens fussed and clucked when Rosalinda took an egg from them. The chicken pecked at Sophia when she tried to get an egg, but it didn't hurt. After a few attempts, she retrieved a speckled, warm egg.

They walked down a path to the orchard. Rosalinda showed the girls where they could find the pecans that had fallen from the trees. They gathered the nuts, talking as they worked. Rosalinda told Sophia how pleased she was that Joshua had decided to send for a wife.

"He is much like you two girls," Rosalinda said. "He's... eh... I don't remember the word in English, he's like *un huerfano*. No mother, no father."

"An orphan?" Sophia asked.

Rosalinda nodded. “Yes, an orphan.”

Sophia wondered if she understood Rosalinda correctly. Last night over dinner, Josh had told them about his mother and stepfather’s home in Houston. He went on to say that his mother didn’t care to visit the country, but one day, perhaps, he’d take Sophia to Houston.

“I might be mistaken, but I believe he told me that he had a mother and stepfather.”

Rosalinda waved a dismissive hand. “His mother doesn’t care about anyone but herself. The stepfather is no better.”

Sophia was taken aback. Rosalinda was undoubtedly devoted to Joshua, but still, her words were very strong. They sounded harsh even to Sophia’s ear. Ginny’s brows raised, but she said nothing, returning instead to the task of collecting pecans.

“I tell you a story,” Rosalinda said. “When I started cooking for Mr. Bentley, he fell off a horse and broke some bones, here.” She gestured to her side.

“His ribs?” Sophia asked.

“Yes, his ribs. Francisco and I write to his mother, saying to her that Mr. Bentley is hurt. She writes us back to say she’s too busy. Too busy? She has one son! I have six. If one of them gets hurt, I go right away.”

Rosalinda shook her head with disgust and tossed a handful of pecans into the basket with a little more force than needed. Sophia’s heart squeezed with pain as she imagined Josh getting badly hurt. If that ever happened again, God forbid, she’d do everything in her power to comfort him. He might only want her to give him an heir, but she prayed he would allow her to care for him if he were to get hurt or become ill.

The three of them filled the basket, chatting amiably as they worked. Two of the cowboys ambled over to say hello and ask Rosalinda what she planned to do with the pecans. They addressed the cook, but Sophia felt their curious glance drift over to her. Their attention irritated her.

"Hello, miss," one of them said to her with a smirk as he tipped his hat. "I didn't know we had company."

Before Sophia could send them on their way, Rosalinda set into them, chiding them for their bad manners and neglecting their chores. They backed away, chuckling and holding up their hands, feigning surrender.

"She's the wife of the jefe," Rosalinda scolded. "You'll call her *Mrs. Bentley*. Not Miss."

When they heard that news, they looked repentant, if not somewhat alarmed. They hurried away. A moment later Josh rode up to the orchard, his expression thunderous.

"Did those boys bother you ladies?" he asked.

Rosalinda replied before Sophia could.

"I sent them away," Rosalinda answered.

Josh's fierce expression faded. He held Sophia's gaze for a long moment. His attention took her by surprise and brought a bloom of warmth to her. While Sophia was used to defending children in the orphanage, she couldn't recall a single time when someone had shown concern for her well-being. She smiled, feeling awkward. He gave her an answering smile.

"I hadn't told the men about my bride," he grumbled, good-naturedly. "Some of them are a little rough around the edges. I'll speak to them about minding their manners around the womenfolk."

"They didn't trouble us," Sophia said. She wanted to tell him that she knew how to defend herself, but realized he saw that as his job. It was a notion she found comforting.

"I'll be along for lunch shortly," he said.

"See you then," Sophia said. She watched him as he rode back to the barnyard.

They resumed filling the basket with nuts. They worked as they chatted about pecan pies and baking in general. Ginny tried to convince Rosalinda to show her how to bake pies and cakes. Rosalinda fussed about having other women in her kitchen, but in the end, she smiled at Ginny and relented.

A voice called from the edge of the orchard. "Yoo-hoo! Is someone there?"

Sophia, Ginny and Rosalinda crossed the orchard. A woman, elegantly attired, sat on the seat of a fine two-wheeled buggy. She held the reins in her gloved hands and regarded them with a haughty expression. "My name is Eleanor Addington. I'm looking for my son, Joshua Bentley. Have you seen him?"

Sophia uttered a small murmur of surprise. "I'm Sophia Bentley. Pleased to meet you, Eleanor."

It was the first time she'd said her married name aloud. It sounded strange to her ear. The woman's eyes widened but her surprise soon faded, and she smiled broadly.

"Hello, dear. You may call me Ellie." Her gaze drifted down Sophia." You're not as much of a tragedy as I feared. What on earth are you doing?"

Sophia didn't know what to make of the woman's words, but decided to ignore any insult, intended or otherwise. Behind her, Ginny muttered something about speaking of the devil.

"We're collecting pecans for a pie."

"How charming." She wrinkled her nose. "It sounds very rustic."

"Have you come for a visit?"

She curled her lip. "How did you guess?"

Behind Sophia, Rosalinda muttered something in Spanish.

Ellie narrowed her eyes and looked past Sophia. "Are you one of Joshua's servants?"

Rosalinda regarded the older woman with a bland look on her face.

"I asked if you're the maid?" Ellie raised her voice. "I need help unpacking. I intend to stay at least a week to make certain that Joshua has matters in hand. I have a dozen or more gowns packed in my trunks. They'll need airing and pressing."

Rosalinda said nothing. Ginny snickered and then, as if realizing her poor manners, coughed to conceal her amusement. The girl's laughter made Sophia realize that Rosalinda was baiting Joshua's mother. Sophia watched in astonishment.

"Hello! Are you deaf?" Ellie demanded.

With this, Rosalinda smiled sweetly and shook her head. She lifted the basket filled with pecans and marched past, giving Ellie a pointed look. "*No hablo ingles*."

Chapter Fourteen

Josh

"I'm not getting an annulment, Mother."

His mother straightened, somehow forcing her ramrod posture into an even more erect stance. They sat in his study, he behind his desk and she in a chair across from him. Her eyes flashed with uncontained fury. She gripped the armrests of the chair so tightly that her knuckles whitened.

"The girl, the little one." She pursed her lips as she pondered. "Minnie?"

"Ginny."

"She told me you sleep in separate rooms."

He shook his head with a look meant to imply a note of warning. "Stop this."

"I don't mean to be indelicate, Joshua."

"Then kindly refrain from discussing Sophia, *my wife*."

"If you haven't become man and wife, then you can still send the girl on the way. I'll give her a parting gift. What would be suitable? A thousand dollars?"

"No."

"Fine. Two thousand dollars and I'll give her an extra five hundred for the little lame girl. I actually rather like her."

Josh sat back in his chair and steepled his fingers. "It's lovely having you here. Such a nice surprise."

"Watch your tone, Joshua."

"I won't allow you to disrespect Sophia."

His mother tilted her head and widened her eyes. "You're fond of the girl after one whole day. I never knew you to be such a romantic. I'd always considered you to be too practical to believe in love at first sight. Although, I will admit, Sarah is quite comely. She has a pretty face and obviously a fine figure."

"Her name is Sophia."

His mother rolled her eyes. "You could have any girl with just a snap of your fingers."

"I don't want any girl. I want the woman I've married. I wanted her before she stepped foot on the train."

"Well, that's heartwarming. It brings a tear to my eye."

"I'm glad you understand. But then again, you've always understood me so well."

"Manners, Joshua."

He shrugged, not caring in the least if his mother understood the depth of his feelings for Sophia. How could he explain when he didn't understand them himself? He forged on, knowing full well that she'd ridicule his attachment to his wife. "I might have only exchanged a few letters with Sophia, and yet, I felt a bond to her from the beginning."

"Very touching. Perhaps you should write poetry about the girl."

He clenched his jaw. "Perhaps I will."

His mother smiled and nodded. "You could start with a limerick."

"There's no need to be bitter, just because you never felt such affection. Love at first sight is hardly your style, is it?"

"Of course, I understand love at first sight. The sight of Niles's bank balance inspired love at first sight. And before you complain, you might recall that his money certainly made your life comfortable."

"You sold my father's property. You had plenty of money."

She waved off his words. "This again. I can see the futility of further discussion, but don't imagine I'm done trying to banish that little tattered street urchin from this home. If you think she returns your affection, you're more foolish than I feared."

Josh laughed. "Say what you want to me, Mother, but insult my wife and I will ask you to leave our home. Sophia is a lady. She might not be perfect. Neither am I, but Sophia is perfect for me."

His mother sniffed, got to her feet and gave him a stern look, her eyes flashing. "I'm going to see what Rosalinda is making for dinner. Despite her sullen manner, I suspect she's a fine cook. It's a shame she doesn't speak English."

Josh tried to fathom what she meant, and then it dawned on him. He schooled his features to conceal his amusement. The aroma of dinner was indeed tantalizing, and, despite his mother's disapproval of everything else, she would have to admit that Rosalinda's cooking was excellent.

With a huff, his mother swept from the room. Josh heaved a sigh of relief. In the past, he'd held a half-hearted wish that his mother might visit. Now he hoped she might cut her visit short. How was he to woo his bride with his embittered mother skulking around his home?

She'd made the trip because his stepfather traveled in Mexico. Niles visited silver mines and could be gone for weeks, maybe months. Did that mean his mother would stay weeks or maybe months? With a groan of frustration, he tried to push the unsettling possibility from his mind.

He crossed the room to add wood to the fireplace. The coals burned low, allowing a chill to creep into the room, or perhaps it was his mother's presence lending a cold nip to his home. He stirred the embers and watched as the flames leapt up, crackling as they ignited the dried mesquite.

"Josh..." His name, whispered behind him, drew his attention to the nearby chesterfield.

Sophia reclined on the cushions, holding a book, and looked at him with an alarmed expression. "I'm sorry," she said softly. "I didn't mean to overhear anything."

He grimaced as he recalled the ugly things his mother had said about Sophia. He should have insisted his mother keep her thoughts to herself. Instead, he'd argued, hoping to sway her opinion. After so many pointless debates, he should have known his mother would never see his view of things.

"Sophia, I'm sorry you heard all that." He set his hand over his heart. "I never, for one moment, have wavered in wanting you to come to Texas."

She sat up, keeping her gaze fixed on him. "Her words don't trouble me. I've faced far worse than a rich, privileged woman who called me a tattered urchin. In a way, she's right about me."

Pain squeezed his heart. "Don't say that about yourself. I'm going to ask her to leave. First thing in the morning, she'll be gone. She can come back after you've settled in. Or we can go visit her in Houston."

She rose from the chesterfield and, to his amazement, her lips curved into a gentle smile. "She loves you, Josh. She just has a poor way of showing it."

Standing before him, clad in a pale yellow, gauzy dress, Sophia looked angelic. She laughed, and a blush of color bloomed across her cheeks. "I didn't care for what she said, but it was worth the unpleasantness."

"What do you mean? How could it have been worth the unpleasantness?"

"I didn't like what she said, of course, but I appreciated your words about me."

"I meant it," he said. "Every word. I'm glad you're here. Sophia, I thank God for bringing you to Texas, for blessing me with such a lovely wife. You look lovely this evening. It warms my heart to know you have pretty things."

With a shy smile, she ran her hands across her skirts. The material rustled under her palms. "Before I came, Mrs. Prescott bought me a dress for the trip."

He frowned. "Just one? I sent plenty of money, so you could buy what you needed for yourself and Ginny too."

"I only needed one dress. We decided on a brown frock. She thought you wanted a plain bride."

He shook his head. "I told her I didn't care one way or another. I meant that I wanted a girl with a good heart. Like you, but you're beautiful too. What happened to your brown dress?"

Sophia laughed softly. "Ginny threw it from the train."

"I don't understand. Everything you've worn has been fancy."

"We met two ladies on the train. Their granddaughter had eloped, leaving behind her trousseau. They gave it to me. Mabel and Gertie were sort of like a pair of fairy godmothers." She gave him a sheepish look. "I suppose they hated the brown dress too."

A surge of irritation singed his veins as he considered that strangers on a train had felt sorry for his wife.

"I should have come for you, Sophia, and then I would have bought you everything you needed."

"And then you might have forbidden me from bringing Ginny."

He shook his head. "I wouldn't have forbidden that."

She looked surprised. "No?"

"Living on a ranch gets lonesome, especially for the women. I've seen that myself. I liked the notion of you having a little company, especially since you two girls are so fond of each other."

"That's very sweet."

She gazed at him in wonder as if he'd presented her with a precious gift. He couldn't begin to explain how he wanted to spend the rest of his days making her happy. To do that he needed to spend time alone with her, away from everyone else. He and Sophia needed moonlit walks, picnics by the stream, long talks sitting on the porch swing.

Her smile faded. "Thank you for saying those things about me, Josh. I'm touched by your words about me being perfect for you. I've never heard anything so sweet, so romantic."

He stepped closer, took her hands in his and held them for a long moment as he gazed into her eyes. "So why do you look unhappy?"

She gave him a wistful look, "Haven't you heard of Cinderella?"

His heart warmed at her playful words, but he heard the note of sadness in her voice. Standing close to her sent a thrill across his senses. A soft floral scent clung to her feminine form. Her skin felt like silk in his work-roughened hand. The shine in her eyes made his heartbeat quicken. He wanted to keep her near him, just like this, forever.

He smiled. "Sophia..."

Her expression grew solemn. “I fear what might happen when the clock strikes twelve.”

“Nothing will change, sweetheart.” He brushed a kiss across her hand. “I won’t ever let you go.”

Chapter Fifteen

Sophia

While Sophia knew that Ellie didn't approve of her, she didn't expect her to confront her directly. A few days after she arrived, Ellie came to her room in the evening just as Sophia was about to prepare for bed. She closed the door behind her and leaned against it, a stern look on her face.

Sophia smiled at her reflection in the mirror and continued brushing her hair.

Ellie folded her arms across her chest. "I think you're hiding something."

"Like what?" Sophia asked, keeping her voice steady.

"I think you're hiding the real reason you came here. Maybe you have a husband back in Boston, one you don't care for. Or a criminal past. I don't know what it is, but I'm certain you had some ulterior motive for coming all this way to marry a stranger."

Sophia schooled her features to remain calm. She hadn't imagined that Ellie would come so close to guessing her secret. She set her brush down and turned to face her. "I did have an ulterior motive, in fact."

"I knew it. And now my poor son is going to have his heart broken."

"I won't break his heart. I care for Josh."

Ellie scoffed.

“When I first went to the bridal broker, I wanted to find a way out of Boston, mostly for Ginny’s sake. She was so unhappy living at the orphanage.”

Ellie didn’t respond, and Sophia wasn’t sure if she believed her or not.

“After Josh wrote me, I lost my nerve.”

“What changed your mind?”

“The boys in the orphanage treated Ginny so unkindly. I tried to protect her, but I couldn’t always keep her safe.”

“Poor Ginny. I never imagined...”

“Not long after, the older ones threatened her. If she didn’t work for them, pickpocketing and petty thievery, they’d make her life difficult.” Sophia’s voice shook with emotion. “As if her life wasn’t difficult enough.”

Ellie sighed and let her arms fall to her sides. Her expression softened, and in the soft lamplight, Sophia could see what a beautiful woman Josh’s mother was when she wasn’t scowling.

“I know you love Josh,” Sophia said. “I promise to take good care of his heart.”

“All right, then. I suppose I’ll have to reconsider my opinion of you.” She turned to leave, pausing by the door. “Perhaps. You’re certain there’s no husband back in Boston?”

Sophia couldn’t hold back a smile. The notion was so absurd, she couldn’t help herself. “No husband. No sweetheart or beau. When Josh and I exchanged vows, he gave me my first kiss.”

Ellie rolled her eyes. “Where did you get married? Please don’t tell me it was the train depot.”

“It wasn’t the train depot.”

“Thank heavens.”

“It was at the gunsmith’s shop.”

Ellie set her hand over her heart. "I should have known better than to ask."

With that, Ellie left. Sophia let out a deep breath, grateful that she'd been able to evade any further questions. She knew she needed to tell Josh. One day she would. In the meantime, she wanted to guard her secret, if only for just a little longer.

The next afternoon, Josh invited her to go riding. She thought about telling him what his mother had said but decided against it. He came to the house with two horses. Sophia met him on the porch, dressed in a divided skirt that Rosalinda had sewed for her. Ginny followed along with Rosalinda.

Ellie came last, hurrying out the door with a pair of leather gloves. "You can't ride without gloves," she fussed. "Not unless you want to have hands as rough as a cowboy's."

Josh lifted her atop the horse like she weighed no more than a sack of flour, and a small sack at that. She gave a small gasp to find herself high above the ground, astride the horse. Josh stood beside her, a mischievous grin lighting his face. He chuckled as he coaxed her fingers around the reins.

"You're a rancher now, Sophia. You need to learn to ride a horse, and Cinders is as gentle and kind as they come."

Caleb, the young ranch hand, ambled over. "Even Josh can ride Cinders."

Josh shook his head. "Don't listen to that smart-mouthed boy. The cowboys like to joke about me getting pitched from a horse. It's only happened a handful of times, and it's because I'm a big fella. That's why I ride Hercules. He's big enough and strong enough to carry me without complaint."

Josh's horse was indeed big, especially compared to Cinders. The horse had a placid, amenable expression on his face. He stood by the hitching rail, his copper coat gleaming in the sunshine.

A small crowd watched, and Sophia felt her face warm with embarrassment. Rosalinda watched from the porch. She looked slightly panicked and, muttering in Spanish, she crossed herself. Ginny stood beside her with a grin on her face, likely hoping that Sophia would meet some unfortunate, but not too unfortunate, calamity.

Ellie looked pale and stricken. "Joshua, do you think this is prudent?"

Josh swung into the saddle of his mount. "I thought you wanted me to get rid of my bride, mother." He winked at Sophia.

"I did, in fact." She gave Sophia a pained smile. "Sorry, dear, it's true."

Sophia knew perfectly well that Ellie wanted Josh to marry someone better than her, but for now she simply wanted to think about staying in the saddle, not defending herself against her mother-in-law's disapproval.

Ellie went on. "But I didn't want you to discard her in a *painful* way."

Josh held a rope, a tether fastened to Cinders' bridle.

"I'm here to stay, Ellie," Sophia said as she tried to reason what to do with the lengths of leather rein.

"I see that," Ellie said. "And what a plucky girl you are."

"I'd like to go riding sometime," Ginny said.

Ginny's feet were bare. Her toes peeped out from under the hem of her dress. Gazing at the horses with a wistful expression on her face, Ginny didn't seem to mind or even notice.

"Where are your boots?" Sophia asked.

Ginny shrugged. “I don’t know. They were muddy so I left them on the back porch. This morning I went to fetch them and give them a good cleaning and they were gone.”

Sophia shook her head. “Who would take your boots?”

“I don’t know.”

“You must have forgotten where you left them.”

Ellie looked aghast. “Virginia, you poor child. Have you only one pair of boots?”

Ginny pursed her lips, her indignation flaring. “Yes, ma’am. I only have one pair of feet.”

Ellie threw her hands in the air. “Heavens. I’ve never heard of such a thing. Come with me. I might have something that fits. I don’t know what you people would do without me! Joshua, you take care with Sophia.”

Ellie ushered Ginny inside with Rosalinda following close behind.

Sophia smiled at Josh. “She’s not offering me heaps of money to leave you.”

“She’s worried I might let something happen to you. Usually, she doesn’t change her mind that quickly. I can’t think of a single instance of that happening. You’ve won her over.”

“I think Ginny has won her over.”

“Ready to go?”

“I suppose we should.”

Josh urged his horse on with a soft command. He led Cinders, who followed obediently. Sophia took in the sight of her husband in his cowboy attire. He wore chaps, boots, spurs with big, shiny rowels, and a cowboy hat. Her husband looked rather handsome. No, he looked *very* handsome, she thought with an inward smile.

They left the barnyard, taking a trail that led through a broad, grassy pasture and made their way to a grove of trees in the distance. The late afternoon sun shone brilliantly, chasing the chill from the air.

"You're different than I imagined," she said. "Warmer hearted."

He arched a brow. "You thought I sounded cold-hearted from my letters? I'm certain that I told you I cared for you and felt a bond to you even without having met you."

She nodded. "You did. You said we were meant to be, but often your letters suggested you wanted a business partner, not a wife."

"I should tell you something. I was engaged once before."

He regarded her with a grim look. His words took her aback and she waited for him to continue, her heart thudding against her ribs.

"It was a girl my mother wanted me to marry. I'd never met a girl I wanted to make my wife, so I went along with her schemes. I figured one girl was as good as another."

"What happened?"

"I lost quite a bit of money in a venture with my stepfather. My fiancée caught wind of my bad luck and told me she was too pretty to be a pauper."

She wasn't sure what surprised her more about his words. A small thread of jealousy wound through her, an ugly feeling she rarely felt, but recognized at once. She must have made her feelings clear, judging from Josh's amusement.

"She meant nothing to me, Sophia. Not like you. You mean the world to me. Even before you came, I cared for you."

Her eyes prickled with unshed tears. She prayed that she wouldn't tear up like a fool and tried to make light of his tender words. "In that case, you're forgiven."

"I wanted a wife that would love the Texas countryside like I do, or at least not complain about living on a ranch."

She couldn't fathom finding fault with this paradise. While she'd lived here only a short while, everything she saw filled her with wonder. Inside his home, she marveled at his collection of ironware and soft luxurious bedding and lovely furnishings. When she stepped outside, the gardens and vistas stole her breath.

"I love your home and your ranch."

"It belongs to both of us. It's *our* home and *our* ranch."

Once again, Sophia felt herself tumbling through some dream. The ranch, the house, and most of all Joshua seemed too good to be true. In truth, the circumstances frightened her. She didn't want to allow herself to be happy for fear that it would all be snatched away from her, and from Ginny too.

They rode along the stream, through the groves of trees and across the pastures. Riding a horse seemed a little easier than she'd imagined, or maybe it was Cinders, her sweet and placid mount. In the distance, an eerie, quavering cry rose, piercing the stillness. The horses pricked their ears.

"What's that noise?" Sophia asked.

"Coyotes. Usually they yip at night."

The ghostly sound drew closer. Cinders snorted and pranced. Out of nervousness, Sophia clutched the reins a little tighter. Josh spoke to the mare in a soothing tone. Suddenly, two deer dashed across their path.

The animals startled the mare. She reared in fright. Sophia grabbed the horse's mane and held on for dear life. When the horse came down, Josh was by her side in an instant. He circled his arm around her waist, ready to lift her off the horse, but the mare quieted.

As quickly as it had started, it was over. Josh held her gaze, his expression somewhere between worry and admiration. Sophia laughed in disbelief, just as astonished as he was.

"That was some excitement," she marveled.

"You're not frightened?"

"Terrified, but at least I didn't fall off like Caleb did."

Josh chuckled. "You're a natural."

Her hands were shaking and yet she felt an overwhelming surge of pride at his words. She'd never troubled herself with what others thought, but it pleased her that he admired her.

"Do you want to go back to the barn?" he asked.

"No, I'm fine."

"My brave bride," he said with a chuckle.

The rest of the afternoon passed without incident. They rode through the pastures, into a valley and along a bright, sparkling stream. Everywhere she looked, Sophia saw visions of pastoral beauty. Trees lined the riverbank, their boughs drooping over the water. The trunks were rough-looking and the roots thick and knobby. They were Montezuma cypress, Josh explained, water-greedy trees that thrived near streams and ponds.

The river gurgled as it swirled across shallow, rocky stretches. When they reached a part of the river where the water flowed quietly, they let the horses drink. In the stillness, Sophia gazed into the depths and saw fish swimming amongst the rocks. The sights and sounds of the river mesmerized her and she was sorry to leave, but the sun dipped in the sky.

When they returned to the barn, Caleb met them and took the horses. Sophia and Josh walked back to the house, hand in hand. She thrilled at his touch and reveled at the way he gazed at her.

"I think that Caleb might be sweet on Ginny," she said quietly.

Josh nodded in agreement. “He offered to come help while my cowboys work the back pastures, but he sure is sticking around longer than usual.”

They ascended the steps and when she reached the top, Josh tugged her elbow, turning her towards him. Even though he was on the step below hers, he stood taller than she did. His scent, a masculine trace, washed over her, making her shiver with an emotion she couldn’t name.

“I don’t like to think about you being in danger, sweetheart,” he said. “I had a bit of a scare when Cinders reared. I’m sorry that happened.”

“It turned out all right,” she said shyly. “I won’t brag about it. Much.”

He cupped her jaw and stroked her cheek with his thumb. “I didn’t expect my mail-ordered bride to be so brave and so pretty.”

She laughed as a slow bloom of warmth wrapped around her heart. “Are you trying to tell me that you’re sweet on me?”

He shook his head. “No.”

She gave his shoulder a playful push. “You’re *not* sweet on me? That’s not very nice of you to say. Especially after I almost met a terrible demise on the back of Cinders.”

He didn’t laugh or even smile at her joke. “Sophia,” he said softly. He took her hand in his and set it on his chest, covering it with his palm. “I’m not a boy like Caleb. I’m a man. I love you with all my heart.”

Her lips parted with surprise and she felt a soft huff leave her throat. He lowered to kiss her, threading his fingers through her hair and cupping the back of her head. Standing on the porch, anyone could see them, but Sophia hardly cared.

Josh’s kiss made her feel as though they were alone in the world, just the two of them. Her mind whirled with the sheer pleasure of his kiss. She sank in his arms, giving herself over to his touch.

A sound from the doorway interrupted their kiss. Rosalinda stood on the threshold, eyes wide and her mouth hanging open. "I'm sorry," she muttered, blushing furiously.

"Time for dinner?" Josh asked.

"In an hour," she said. "I wanted to tell you that I know what happened to Ginny's boots. I saw Caleb on the back porch. I think he might have taken her boots."

Josh grumbled, a low indistinct growl of displeasure. "That doesn't make any sense. Why would he take her boots?"

Rosalinda shrugged. "I don't know. Anyway, it doesn't matter. Your mother gave her a new pair." She sniffed and gave a look of disdain. "Fancy boots that Ginny likes very much. She won't mind if Caleb has done something with her old boots."

With that, Rosalinda returned to her duties in the kitchen.

"Josh," Sophia murmured. "You shouldn't kiss me on your front porch."

He shook his head, a smile tugging at his lips as he led her inside. "I'll kiss you wherever I like."

Chapter Sixteen

Josh

The next morning, Josh found Sophia in the yard working in Rosalinda's garden. His cook didn't grow much of a winter garden, just some carrots, cabbage and chard. Josh watched from the back porch, wondering what Sophia was doing. He couldn't for the life of him understand why his bride toiled with a garden spade, turning over the earth as if preparing to plant.

Even more bewildering was the question of why his sweet wife did the work that one of his men should be doing for her. Stubborn girl. He recalled how she and Ginny had hauled the trunks upstairs when they first arrived.

"Sophia," he called. "You shouldn't be doing that. I'll have one of the men work the garden for you, sweetheart."

She smiled at him and brushed a loose tendril of hair from her eyes. "I'm enjoying myself immensely. I asked Rosalinda if we could plant anything soon. I'm eager to get my hands in the dirt."

"I reckon she said we need to wait till May."

"She said we could plant potatoes mid-February. I'm going to have the garden ready by then."

He crossed the yard and took the spade from her hands. Her face glowed with happiness, but he couldn't stand the notion of his wife working like a common laborer. At least she protected her hands with gloves. He could just imagine his mother's response to Sophia doing men's work with bare hands. She'd likely faint.

Ginny came out of the house and made her way across the yard, her limp pronounced and painful looking. Josh tried not to wince. Ginny stopped at the edge of the garden and lifted the hem of her skirt a couple of inches to show off her boots.

"Mrs. Addington gave me a pair of her boots. I'm almost afraid to wear them."

"My mother is fond of you, isn't she?" Josh asked, setting to work digging the garden.

Just then Caleb came around the corner of the house, whistling. He stopped when he saw them, but his lips curved into a happy grin. He held Ginny's old boots in his hand.

Ginny set her hands on her waist. "Why you rascal, Caleb Bentley. What are you doing with my boots?"

He gestured to the porch stairs. "Come sit down. See if you like what I did to your boots."

Giving him a skeptical look, Ginny did as he instructed.

"Take off those boots and try these ones on."

"You're mighty bossy," she grumbled.

Josh had no idea what Caleb was up to. Sophia didn't seem to either, and when she gave him an inquisitive look, he shrugged in response. He set the spade aside. They went to the steps to see what Caleb had in store for Ginny.

She put on her old boots, laced them and stood up. She gave a soft gasp. "Why, Caleb, you gave the one a little bit of a heel."

"I did. I figured you could try it out and if you don't care for the feel of it, I can take it right back off."

With an astonished expression, Ginny walked around the garden. She had no discernable limp and walked as smoothly as if she'd never suffered any injury. Her eyes shone as if she might burst into tears. Sophia felt her eyes prickle too.

"Caleb, that was a mighty good idea," Josh said. To his embarrassment, his voice was choked with emotion. Fortunately, no one seemed to notice. Everyone watched Ginny walk unhindered by her old injuries.

A few minutes later, Rosalinda and his mother ventured out of doors. They too marveled at Caleb's handiwork. His mother gave him Ginny's new pair and asked him to make the necessary adjustments to them.

"I can if Ginny wants me to," Caleb said, blushing.

"If it's not too much trouble," Ginny replied.

"Why, it's no trouble at all." Caleb tucked the boots under his arm and went back to the barn shed.

"It seems like a miracle," Ginny murmured.

Josh draped his arm over Sophia's shoulders and tugged her closer. It did seem like a miracle. He wished he'd thought of it first. He wanted to make Ginny's life better, and it was a love-sick youngster who had the remedy. It was heartwarming to see Caleb's happy grin.

Chapter Seventeen

Sophia

That afternoon, dark clouds gathered on the horizon. Josh spent much of the time in the barnyard, working on repairs and preparing for his men to return from the back pastures. Rosalinda made a pitcher of lemonade. Sophia took him a glass. The gesture earned her a broad smile, one that made her heartbeat quicken.

"Thank you, pretty girl. I'll kiss you later. I'm too dusty now."

The hungry look in his eye sent a jolt of awareness across her senses. Her lips felt pleasantly warm and tingly as she imagined him giving her a long, lingering kiss. Her cheeks burned. She tried to brush away the turmoil of her thoughts and turned her attention to the threatening sky.

"Do you think we'll get a storm?"

"We could use some rain."

"Your mother told me that the rain is different here in Texas, more of a torrential downpour than what we have on the east coast."

He wiped his brow. "Our storms can get violent. And the rain comes down in buckets."

She shivered. "Are you coming in soon, then?"

"I'm expecting my men soon. They went to the northern pastures to round up a herd of rogue bulls."

"Rogues?"

"Right. We have a few dozen young, ornery bulls that we've kept away from the main herd. They were fighting the older bulls. I need to sell them, pronto." Josh drained his glass and gave it back to her. "They're dangerous."

"Dangerous?"

"That's right."

"Like the coyotes?"

"Worse."

"What's the most dangerous thing around here?"

He grinned at her, drew closer and lowered his voice. "You're looking at him."

She shook her head with mild reproach but couldn't hold back a smile. They held each other's gaze for a lingering moment. Her heart fluttered. She felt lost in his eyes. One day soon, the two of them would begin their lives as man and wife. To her surprise, she realized she yearned for his touch and wanted to be his completely.

"I love you, Sophia," he said quietly, lifting his palm to her jaw. "With all my heart."

"I love you, too," she whispered.

He lowered and brushed a kiss across her lips.

His tenderness made her defenses fall. She wanted to confess to him about the time she'd been caught with the stolen wallet. She wanted to lay her shame out in the open in hopes he'd forgive her. The secret she held felt like a terrible burden. "I want to tell you something."

He gazed at her, his smile never faltering. She was about to speak when a noise drew her attention. The cowboys returned with the cattle. Dust billowed in the distance. Riders and cattle spread across the horizon. The rumble of hooves over the parched ground wafted on the breeze, growing louder.

"You go on, Sophia." He kissed her on the forehead. "We'll talk later."

"All right." She turned to the house, feeling a sense of unease. She'd been close to unburdening her heart, but circumstances prevented her from saying what she needed to say. Somehow, the weight on her conscience had doubled. She walked to the house, her eyes downcast.

"Sophia!"

Josh's voice yanked her from her distress. The herd drew closer now. Leading the herd was a single bull. He charged ahead of the herd, heading straight to her. His nostrils flared. When he lowered his head, his horns glinted in fading sunlight.

She set off in a run, heading for the house as quickly as her feet would carry her. Josh yelled again, taunting the bull, drawing the animal's attention from her. She glanced back. Josh stalked across the barnyard directly to the charging beast.

"Josh!"

"Go!" he roared.

The bull changed course and charged directly at Josh. Sophia sprinted the rest of the way to the house and raced up the steps. When she reached the top, she searched the barnyard for Josh. Dust billowed, rising to the sky. Just a moment before, the barnyard had been empty. Now the herd streamed into the barnyard, kicking up thick, choking sand. The cowboys flanked the herd. They whistled and shouted, either to each other or to the cattle.

Where was Josh?

The bulls snorted and tussled. A shout rose up. More yelling followed. Through the confusion, Sophia heard Caleb's voice. His words sent a chill through her heart.

Josh's been hurt...

She gripped the porch railing, hardly daring to breathe. Francisco swung a bullwhip over his head. Over and over he cracked it. While he didn't whip the animals, they seemed eager to move away. He pushed them to the corral. One of his men slammed the gate. A veil of dust hung in the air and Sophia could see nothing.

A moment later, Francisco loped across the yard. He stopped in front of the house and swiped his hat from his head. His grim expression terrified her.

"Mr. Bentley have a small problem with a bull."

"Tell me he's all right," she whispered.

Rosalinda hurried out of the house and spoke to her husband in a panicked flurry of Spanish. After what seemed an eternity, Francisco nodded goodbye and rode off.

Rosalinda turned to face her. "They're taking him to Magnolia. Mr. Bentley says you need to stay here. He doesn't want you to see his..."

"His what?"

Rosalinda raised a trembling hand and pointed to her shoulder. "The bull give him a small cut."

Out in the barnyard, Josh's cowboys helped him into the saddle of one of the horses. From where she stood, she couldn't make out his injury, but if he needed help mounting a horse, it had to be bad.

"I should go with him," Sophia exclaimed. "I'm his wife."

Rosalinda waved a dismissive hand. "Josh is very tough. I see him get run over by a bull and get right back up. You will see. He will be fine."

With Francisco at his side, Josh rode off. She watched him until he disappeared, then turned away and hurried inside. How could this be happening? Just a moment ago, he'd held her and told her he loved her. Now he was hurt. Not only was he hurt, but he didn't want her help. She found Ellie upstairs in her room, reclining on a chaise, a book on her lap. She set the book aside, and got to her feet, a smile curving her lips. "Dinnertime, already?"

Sophia shook her head.

Ellie narrowed her eyes and crossed the room, stopping a few steps away. "Sophia, what's wrong."

"Josh is hurt."

"What happened?"

"There was a bull. It was coming for me. Josh distracted it."

"Merciful heaven," Ellie whispered.

"They're taking him to Magnolia. He doesn't want me..." Sophia's words trailed off. "He doesn't want me to come."

Chapter Eighteen

Josh

Despite his injury, Josh managed to stay seated in the saddle. He gripped the pommel and clenched his jaw. He said a prayer of thanks that the bull decided to come after him and not Sophia.

They made the trip quickly, loping most of the way. Dusk gave way to nightfall. The storm that threatened earlier skirted the distant hills. For once, Josh was grateful a storm passed by. On the outskirts of town, they pulled their horses to a trot. Josh grimaced from the agony. Each time his horse's hooves hit the ground, a jolt of pain shot down his side.

"I think the bleeding is less," said Francisco.

"I've ruined my chaps," Josh grumbled. "Doc Williams better be in, or we'll have made the trip for nothing. We could have just tended to this at home."

Francisco shook his head. "I've seen too many vaqueros bleed to death. You don't know how deep." He scowled and gestured at the wound.

"He just hooked me a little, right below the ribs. It's nothing. I don't know when my foreman turned into nursemaid."

Francisco's frown faded. "Every vaquero in Magnolia wants to work on a Bentley Ranch."

"Meaning what?"

“Meaning we want to keep you alive. You’re a good boss.”

His foreman’s words gave him a small respite from the pain. Pride flickered inside him. It was true. Josh and his Bentley cousins ran top-notch outfits and paid their men better than any other ranch boss around. Their men might be a rough and rowdy crowd, but they were loyal.

“You made sure the men won’t bring Sophia, didn’t you?” Josh asked.

“I did.”

“I don’t want her to see me like this. Hurts a man’s pride.”

When they arrived at the doctor’s infirmary, a small clapboard house on the main street, it appeared the doctor was still at work. Francisco hitched the horses. Josh staggered into the office. An orderly had seen him from the window and rushed to help him. They found the doctor in the back, sitting in a chair, arms folded, his eyes closed and snoring loudly.

“William, you better not be drunk,” Josh growled.

The doctor startled and snapped his head up. “What’s that?”

“I said you’d better be sober. I need you to do a little sewing.” Josh paused to catch his breath. Each step sent a wave of pain through his body. The orderly tried to help as best he could, but Josh was a head taller than the young man.

With a groan, Josh limped across the examining room. “I want your stitches to be straight and tidy.”

The doctor rose from the chair, wincing as he rubbed his lower back. “That’s right. I heard you got yourself a bride. You worried about getting uglier?” Dr. Bennet crossed the room and patted the examining table. “Let’s have a look.”

“That’s right. We’re newlyweds, so I need to keep myself as handsome as ever.”

Dr. Bennet frowned at Josh's wound as he helped him to the table. "A bull caught you?"

"That's right." Josh's voice was a rasp as he lay back on the wooden table.

"How long ago?"

"Less than half an hour."

The doctor got to work at once. He tore Josh's shirt off. After he examined the wound, he grimaced. "I delivered three babies today. I was about to call it a day, and then you had to go wrestle a longhorn. Don't you know it's supper time?"

Josh closed his eyes. "I do." He tried to keep from flinching as the doctor examined his side. "A few stitches, and I'll be on my way."

The doctor spoke to his orderly. Josh noted the man's voice sounded far away. It echoed distantly and he couldn't understand anything. The edges of his awareness blurred. Sophia's face appeared in the mist of his thoughts. She smiled at him, her gray eyes shining with happiness.

"Sophia," he whispered. "Sophia..."

Chapter Nineteen

Sophia

Sophia paced the length of the porch. She kept her gaze fixed on the road, searching for a sign of Francisco or Josh. Sometime after dusk, Rosalinda tried to tempt her with a plate of dinner, but Sophia had no appetite. Ginny kept her company, sitting quietly on a bench. Ellie mostly remained in her room. She appeared at nightfall, pale and trembling, to ask if Sophia had heard anything.

"Nothing," Sophia replied.

"I'm sorry that I'm no help to you," Ellie said. "I faint at the sight of blood. Just the thought makes my stomach turn."

"Why don't you lie down? I'll tell you the moment I have news."

Ellie nodded and wandered back inside.

Dreadful thoughts drifted through Sophia's mind. The darkest of her fears left her wondering if she'd ever see her husband again. Perhaps he'd been mortally injured, leaving her a widow before she'd had a chance to be a wife. While she hadn't come to Texas with a strong desire to be a wife, she hadn't imagined marrying a man like Josh either.

Somewhere in the pastures, a coyote yipped. She stopped to listen. A chorus of yips and howls followed. The eerie sounds added to the desolation weighing heavily in her heart.

Her desperation grew as the night wore on. Josh had left without so much as a word, making it perfectly clear he didn't want her by his side in his moment of need. In the days since she'd come to Magnolia, they'd drawn closer than she imagined could be possible. He was warm and kind, but warmth and kindness didn't mean he needed her.

Close to midnight, Ginny rose and headed inside, pausing in the doorway. "You won't be any use to Josh if you don't get some rest."

Sophia nodded. "All right."

She followed Ginny upstairs and got ready for bed. A wave of exhaustion came over her as she lay down, but sleep wouldn't come. In the darkness, she tried to calm her frantic thoughts.

We were meant to be...

His words rang in her ears. She prayed, begging God to watch over Josh. She prayed for his recovery, and for the doctor who tended to him. Throughout the night she implored Him to give her a chance to be a proper wife and, perhaps, one day a mother.

After a restless night, she tossed the covers aside, washed and dressed. She searched through Emily's trousseau, looking for something suitable for what she had planned. She picked a dress with a light, wool weave, one that would shield her from the cold, but not be overly warm as the day wore on. She brushed her hair and arranged it in a simple twist.

She selected a suitable bonnet and at the last moment plucked a parasol from the trunk. She'd never used one in Boston. It was sturdy and serviceable, not that she was terribly concerned about the bright sunshine. What worried her was the chance she might run into coyotes. She envisioned them as big and as fearsome as wolves. She'd never seen a coyote, or a wolf for that matter. How big were they?

Dismissing her fears, she tucked the parasol under her arm. If she ran into one or an entire pack, she'd dispatch them somehow. Back in Boston, she was known for her fearlessness, she reminded herself. The coyotes had better watch out for her!

Stepping out of her room, she listened intently. The house was quiet. She tiptoed down the steps and slipped out the door. As she crossed the porch, the wooden slats creaked beneath her step. Her heart crashed against her ribs. If Rosalinda or Ellie heard her, they'd put a stop to her plans. Of that she was certain.

With care and stealth, she descended the steps. When she reached the bottom, she let out a deep sigh. Now that she'd gotten out of the house without anyone noticing, she needed to make certain she walked in the right direction.

The day Josh had picked her and Ginny up from the train station wasn't much more than a misty memory. She'd been far too worried about marriage to pay attention to the road. Magnolia lay to the east. That much she knew. The morning star shone low in the eastern sky. She gave thanks for the beacon, and for the cloudless night.

Armed with her parasol, reckless resolve, and a fierce devotion to her husband, Sophia set out on the dark road. Josh wouldn't be pleased. Not at all. Once she knew for certain that he was well, she'd set about making amends.

Chapter Twenty

Josh

Vaguely aware of his surroundings, Josh woke every so often to find Francisco peering at him, his face shrouded in shadowed candlelight. His foreman regarded him with alarm, his brow furrowed with worry, his lips pressed to a thin line. Josh woke from a fevered dream to find that dawn had broken. Beside the bed, his foreman slumped in his chair, snoring.

The acrid scent of liniment hung in the air, or perhaps it was a salve on his bandage. The sheets, heavily starched, chafed his skin as he shifted in bed. When he groaned, Francisco woke with a start.

Josh grimaced. “You don’t make a pretty nurse.”

Francisco chuckled and leaned forward in his chair. He set his elbows on his knees and regarded him with a grin. For some reason, the foreman’s good humor irked Josh. He frowned and muttered a few mild curse words.

Francisco’s grin widened, his smile reaching his eyes. The man’s visage usually had a hard-bitten look. He rarely smiled. Like his father and his grandfather, Francisco had spent his life on the back of a horse, shivering in the winter, sweltering in the summer.

“You were talking all night, jefe,” Francisco said. “At least now you make a little sense.”

“What was I talking about?”

"About *your* jefe." Francisco gave a hearty laugh and slapped his knee. A plume of dust rose from his trousers.

"I don't have a boss." Josh pointed his thumb towards his chest, taking care not to make any sudden movement. "I *am* the boss."

Francisco's smile faded. "You should have been on a horse. You knew we were coming with the *toros.* I pretty sure I tell you that before. I'm just going to tell Mrs. Bentley when you take a chance. Maybe you listen to your *esposa*, no?"

"Lost track of time. I was courting my bride." Josh closed his eyes and felt his lips tug into a smile. Warm thoughts drifted across his mind as he thought about Sophia. "I gotta get home," he muttered. "I need to see her."

"The doc said he'd see you this morning. Maybe he will say you can go home. Maybe no."

Josh kept his eyes closed and sank deeper into the bedding. "You should go on, Francisco. Get a little rest. I'll send for you when I need you."

Francisco murmured a few words of farewell as Josh felt himself give in to his exhaustion. Thankfully, he dreamed of Sophia, wonderful, sweet escapes where she let him pull her into his arms and hold her near. Her voice came to him, soft and feminine. She appeared amidst his misty thoughts, standing in the doorway.

"I couldn't stay away," she said softly. "Don't be angry with me."

"How could I be angry?"

She smiled and blinked back tears. For some peculiar reason she held a parasol. He'd never seen her carry one, but his dreams presented such odd images.

"You have a parasol?" He teased the Sophia of his dreams.

She smiled and jabbed it in the air as she crossed the room. "I brought it to fend off the coyotes."

"Seems perfectly reasonable."

"It worked perfectly. I didn't see or hear a single coyote."

Her soft laughter was a balm to his heart. She drew near. He patted the side of the bed, an invitation to come closer. "I want you beside me."

"But you're injured."

"On the other side. It doesn't hurt, though. Doc did a good job."

She set aside her parasol, slipped off her boots and cautiously lowered beside him. He wrapped his arm around her shoulders. She rested her head on his shoulder. His dream seemed so very real. The familiar rustle of her petticoats. The pleasing scent of her floral soap. "Sophia," he said. "Dreaming of my bride is the best medicine."

Chapter Twenty-One

Josh

Rosalinda and Ellie quarreled about the biscuits.

In the last ten minutes, their voices had grown louder. His mother was trying to tell Rosalinda how to make fluffy biscuits. Rosalinda argued in colorful, impassioned Spanish. His mother dispensed demands in crisp and forceful English.

Josh sat at his desk checking his ranch ledger. He sighed, lifted his gaze to Ginny and Sophia. The two of them sat by the window. Sophia had ordered a gardening book from a mail-order company and pored over the pages. She hardly noticed the uproar.

Ginny had been reading too, but now she grinned mischievously just as she did every time the two women squabbled. “Shall I ask if Mrs. Addington wants to take a walk before dinner?”

“Good idea,” he said. “I’d appreciate it.”

The girl flounced out of the room, her smile even wider than a moment before. Probably because she hoped to run into Caleb while walking with his mother. Caleb and Ginny seemed especially fond of each other. Caleb told him that he was determined to make something of himself so that he might call on Ginny one day.

His words surprised Josh. He wasn’t sure what he thought about a boy of eighteen making plans to marry a girl of fifteen.

They both seemed so young. Fortunately, Caleb understood the need to have something to offer a girl.

A moment later, the house grew quiet. He could imagine Rosalinda grumbling under her breath. She hardly allowed anyone in her kitchen for this very reason, but his mother had always seen it as her duty to instruct everyone.

“If we’re going to add trees to the orchard, we should plant sometime soon,” Sophia said, absentmindedly. She looked up from her book and knit her brow. “Where did Ginny go?”

“She’s walking with my mother. If you want to plant fruit trees, I can dig holes in the orchard.”

“I can dig a hole, Josh. Besides, you still need to mend. The doctor said no riding for two weeks. I’m sure he wouldn’t want you to exert yourself.”

Josh leaned back in his chair. He was about to explain that he was perfectly fine, and he wouldn’t sit idle while his wife worked like a field hand. Sophia set the book aside and crossed the room, her expression solemn. He half-expected her to fuss about his injury.

Instead, she closed the door of his study. “I need to tell you something.”

“This isn’t going to be about peach trees, is it?”

“No. It’s a confession, I suppose, something I should have told you before I came. A year ago, I was arrested for theft. I was accused of stealing a man’s wallet. I went to jail for three days.”

His heart thudded heavily in his chest. “All right.”

“Don’t you want to know if I stole it?”

“If you feel like telling me.”

“I stole it.”

She remained motionless, leaning against the door. Her breathing came faster than it normally did, making her chest rise and fall with clear distress. He wanted to go to her. Would she want him to take her in his arms after her confession? Or would she see that as a sign of pity?

"I wanted the money to leave Boston with Ginny."

"I understand."

"The judge ordered I remain behind bars for a month if I couldn't pay the fine. But they released me after three days."

"What happened?"

"At first, I thought they'd reduced the sentence because I wasn't of age. Then I found out someone had paid my fine."

Josh got to his feet and moved toward Sophia, stopping a few paces away. "Who paid the fine?"

Sophia bit her lip. She blinked as her eyes filled with tears. Josh closed the distance between them and brushed her tears away.

"We all have a past, Sophia. No one could blame you for what you did. I was a perfect hellion when I was a boy. I caused all sorts of trouble, not to help anyone, but because I liked behaving badly."

He kissed her forehead and pulled her into his arms. The tension in her shoulders ebbed. She let him hold her and caress her back. "I'm glad you told me. Not because I needed to know, but because I think it was a burden you carried, one you should never have had to shoulder."

She let out a deep, trembling sigh. "Ginny paid the fine. When she found out where I was, she sold her hair. It was long and glorious, and she sold it to buy my freedom."

Sorrow welled in his chest. The thought of Ginny and Sophia, alone in such an uncertain and cruel world, grieved him deeply. They were here now, he told himself. They were safe and happy and he'd be certain to keep them safe and happy.

Chapter Twenty-Two

Sophia

Ellie, sitting across the dining table, offered a tepid smile. "Joshua, please tell your cook that the dumplings are adequate."

Josh grimaced, probably hoping that Rosalinda couldn't hear the lukewarm praise.

Sophia laughed softly but didn't say a word. It wouldn't earn her any points with either woman if she complimented Rosalinda's cooking. Instead, she ate a bite of the savory chicken. Ginny caught her attention and winked at her.

Ellie went on. "I misspoke earlier. I don't care to apologize to Rosalinda since it's not her place to expect an apology, but the least I can do is praise the dish, despite its uninspired qualities. Chicken and dumplings. Not exactly elegant dining."

A crash reverberated in the kitchen.

"Oh dear," Ellie murmured. "That wasn't very silencio, was it?"

Josh muttered a few words of response and turned his attention to Sophia. He covered her hand with his and gave her a small squeeze. "You like it? Chicken and dumplings are a southern dish. It's one of my favorites. Probably why Rosalinda made it. She's been trying to spoil me ever since I had that run-in with the bull."

"It's delicious," Sophia said, avoiding Ellie's gaze.

Ginny agreed as she helped herself to another serving.

Ellie sighed wearily. "I intend to leave in a few days."

Sophia gave a soft murmur of surprise. She was so used to Ellie's presence and could hardly imagine the house without her. She and Ellie hadn't started off on the right foot, but they were on very good terms now. "We'll be sorry to see you go."

"Thank you, dear. I must admit I've enjoyed myself, but when Niles set off for Mexico, I arranged to travel east."

"Gosh, we'll miss you," Ginny said.

Ellie smiled. "Well, maybe you'd like to come with me? It would be an adventure for the two of us. Josh and Sophia can have a little time together. You and I can explore a hotel I've never visited. Would you like that?"

Ginny drew a sharp breath. Her eyes sparkled with excitement. "I like adventure."

"What do you mean by adventure?" Josh asked, his voice gruff.

Ellie frowned. "Don't get that mother-hen tone with me, Joshua. I'm not going to sell her to a circus, for heaven's sake."

Josh pushed his plate aside. "It seems we might have talked privately before you brought the subject up at the dinner table. I might not approve."

Ginny's jaw dropped, and she blinked in surprise. Sophia almost laughed at her response. The girl had been so absorbed in her new life here, not to mention Caleb Bentley, she hadn't realized that Josh cared deeply about her well-being.

Ellie scoffed. "It's nothing scandalous, Joshua. I plan to travel to a hotel known for its therapeutic mineral springs. I'd like to have Ginny along, not just for her company, but so she can avail herself of the springs. They say that Thomas Jefferson stayed there in 1818. The minerals did wonders for his rheumatism."

Sophia found her proposition astonishing. She couldn't imagine being parted from Ginny. They'd been together for years and had forged a bond as fierce and strong as any she'd known. Her stomach churned. It wasn't for her to give permission or withhold it.

"Joshua," his mother said soothingly. "It's just for a few weeks. I'll take care of her as if she were my own."

"Somehow, that doesn't give me much confidence, Mother."

"Oh, pooh. I would have taken you on trips if you hadn't been such a wild little heathen."

Josh shook his head and Sophia heard what sounded like a low rumble coming from him. Her husband *growled.* She pressed her lips together to keep from smiling. Ellie might have her ways, but she cared for Ginny in a way that filled Sophia's heart with tenderness and appreciation. But so did Josh. She was certain that he considered permission for Ginny's trip his to give or withhold.

Ellie went on. "With Niles in Mexico, I have no one to keep me company." She set her hand over her heart. "Ginny will keep me from missing him so terribly."

Josh snorted. "Mother, please."

"Furthermore, The Homestead is in *Virginia.*" Ellie's lips curved with a victorious smile. "I made the travel plans last month. So, you can clearly see that Ginny should come. It was meant to be."

Josh scrubbed a hand down his face and groaned. "I'll give it some thought."

Ginny's face lit with happiness and the sight of the girl's joy spread warmth across Sophia's heart. Josh did not have much faith in Ellie's abilities. But Sophia did. She was certain that the girl would be in good hands. The trip seemed like a fine idea. Not only would Ellie care for her, there was the possibility that the mineral springs would help Ginny in some way.

Later that evening, after the family had retired, Sophia thought about Josh's response to her confession. And she considered the possibility of Ginny traveling to the springs. Josh was caring. She knew he was worried and wanted to keep both her and Ginny safe. In the quiet of her room, she undressed, bathed and donned her gown. Her heart brimmed with love for her taciturn but kind-hearted husband. She smiled as she recalled the glum expression he wore while his mother laid out the details of her trip.

Sophia's heart yearned to be near him, for his touch, his smile and his sweet protective embrace. He was close. She needed to be near him. She cracked the door and listened. The house was quiet. Tiptoeing down the hallway, she felt her heartbeat race. He was injured. There seemed to be a tacit agreement that they'd wait.

There was no rush.

And yet she needed to feel his arms around her.

When she reached his door, her courage flagged. What was she doing, really? The night she'd walked the five miles to Magnolia, arrived at the hospital and laid beside him in the hospital bed, her actions had been those of a concerned wife. And now?

She raised her hand, curled her fingers to knock, but after a long, indecisive moment, let her hand fall to her side. He might be resting. Or in pain. She should return to her bedroom. She was no better than a fool for coming to his room, seeking his touch and perhaps even his kiss.

"Heavens," she exclaimed.

With a rush of abject mortification, she realized that she had said the word aloud. Dear, merciful Lord. He had to have heard! She clapped a hand over her mouth.

She stood rooted to the spot. With horror, she listened to his approaching footsteps. He opened the door, tugged her inside his room, and shut the door. He wrapped her in a warm embrace as he traced a line of kisses across her neck.

“Finally,” he said softly. “My sweet Sophia. The answer to my prayers.”

Epilogue

Four years later...

Caleb Bentley

Rich folk didn't care much for dust blowing about, Caleb noted. The clang of his horse's shoes echoed across the cobbled street. The cobblestones looked as though someone scrubbed them twice a day.

He rode through the fancy part of Houston, feeling out of place. Instead of a fine, pedigreed, dappled gray, he rode a rugged buckskin mustang. Instead of a suit and tie, he wore his cowboy attire, jeans and chambray shirt, chaps, boots and his trusty Stetson.

A man and woman perched in a buggy drove by, coats pulled up high so only parts of their faces were visible.

"Mornin'," Caleb called with a cordial nod.

They ignored him, both keeping their gaze fixed at a point down the road. They passed without even a glance.

A moment later, a woman appeared in the doorway of a house nestled close to the street. The house was smaller than its neighbors, but still was huge compared to what a family needed for sleeping and eating.

Caleb nodded. "Hello, ma'am." The young woman gasped and scurried inside, retreating to the safety of her home. He looked behind and to the side of his horse to see if there was something scary near him, but there was nothing.

"Dang. Reckon I shoulda shaved," he muttered. "Not easy when you're pushing five hundred head of cattle."

For the last five days he'd ridden the lead position all the way to the Houston stockyards. The trip had been hampered by rain. Caleb wanted to look spruced up for today, but the best he'd managed was a dip in an icy stream and a fresh shirt. Unfortunately, that had been two days ago.

It couldn't be helped. He needed to talk to Ginny. Pronto. In the last week, his life had changed in a way he couldn't have imagined. He hoped that meant her life would change too, if she was willing.

A servant appeared on the front step of a large brick home. Under her arm she carried a rolled-up rug. She leaned over the railing and shook it out. Buddy, his horse, walked unperturbed. Some horses might spook at the sight or sound of a carpet flapping, but not his buckskin. Caleb had trained him well.

The horse didn't have an ornery bone in his body, not like when Caleb bought him a few years back. At first, Buddy was scared of his own shadow. It wasn't his fault. The horse had been mistreated. Caleb earned his trust, patiently building it over time. Eventually the horse grew calmer. Nowadays, nothing spooked him.

Plenty of folks wanted to buy the buckskin, but Caleb refused all offers. There was blood and sweat invested in Buddy, and time, hours and hours teaching him how to be a good work horse. His attachment was strong to all the animals he trained, and he never wanted to part with them. Maybe he was tender-hearted, but he didn't like the idea of another cowboy treating his horses harshly. The way to keep them safe was simply to keep them.

He might be a rich man if he bought and sold horses, but there were some things in life more precious than a few extra coins for your pocket. He was a simple man. He didn't need much for himself, but one hard truth remained. If he wanted a wife and family, he'd need more than a cowboy's wages.

His father had plenty of land and could have set him up, but Caleb didn't want that either. He wanted to make it on his own. Or he had wanted to make it on his own. After last week, he'd been forced to reconsider. He reached inside his coat and patted the letter in his breast pocket. When he read the letter, he knew beyond a shadow of a doubt, he would embark on a new path.

Especially since there was an ugly rumor floating around that Mrs. Addington intended to marry Ginny off to some highfalutin banker type. Mrs. Addington made it clear, she wanted to keep Ginny under her protective wing and that meant Ginny marrying a man from Houston. Caleb gritted his teeth. That, he vowed, would not be happening.

He and Ginny were meant to be.

The two hadn't always gotten along perfectly well, truth be told. When she first came to Magnolia, she delighted in playing pranks on him. It started out harmlessly. She'd squeezed half a lemon in his water during dinner at Josh and Sophia's. From across the table, she watched him with wicked delight, as he tried to keep from gasping and sputtering.

Then she stole his boots from the bunkhouse and left a note from the kidnappers. The worst prank had been the letter from President Harrison. The letter, which was on fine stationery and tucked in an even finer envelope, expressed a desire, by the president himself, that Caleb come to Washington to train his finest horse, a Tennessee Walker.

Caleb had been beyond proud. The president wanted him! Caleb had walked around with the letter in his pocket and read it to anyone who would listen. She'd let him brag about it for a day or so, before confessing to having penned the letter herself.

While Caleb had no trouble taming an incorrigible bronc or rogue bull, Ginny could play a trick on him as easy as pie. Probably because of her wide blue eyes, and her smile that turned him into a fool.

Tired of being hoodwinked by a girl three years younger than him, he'd fussed at her, threatening terrible, uncertain retribution. Ginny set aside her tricks. After that they'd gotten along much better.

He smiled, thinking about how he'd taught her the two-step at the wedding of a ranch hand.

While he held her in his arms, she told him that he'd made their dancing possible since he fixed her boots. She could walk and dance just like any other girl. Her eyes shone in a way he had never seen before. She'd been sixteen then and he nineteen. His heart had soared that night as he imagined a life with Ginny, the only girl he'd ever wanted.

That night, three years ago, they were still too young.

Not anymore.

Now he was twenty-two and she was nineteen. He was done waiting. Especially if other fellas thought they were going to call on his girl. Not only were some of the young bucks here in Houston vying for Ginny's attention, but Eleanor Addington seemed to lay a claim to Ginny as well.

Ginny cared for Mrs. Addington. He knew that. The woman's husband was gone all the time, and she claimed to be lonesome. Ginny wanted to care for her, but often when he caught sight of Ginny at Josh's ranch, she looked a little lost. He wanted to offer for her and make a life with her.

But first, before he could even propose, he had to deal with the one woman who stood in the way. Caleb clenched his jaw. Mrs. Addington liked to look down her nose at folks, especially him.

He turned his horse down the final street where the Addington home sat surrounded by magnolias and roses. It was the biggest house. Naturally. She was proud and vain and probably bought the house because it was twice the size of the other homes.

Two women strolled down the street. One was elderly, and the other was much younger, probably a grandmother walking with her granddaughter. Both peered at him from under the brim of wide, plumed hats.

"Howdy," Caleb said with a polite nod. They swept their gazes away from him, pointedly ignoring his greeting. After he passed, he shook his head and muttered, "Howdy, dang it!"

His horse flicked his ears back at the sound of his voice. Caleb grinned and patted his neck. "Atta way, Buddy. I'm glad you got some manners."

Caleb stopped the horse in front of the wrought iron gate and tied his horse to one of the thick railings. He pushed the gate open and went up the expansive steps. To his surprise, Mrs. Addington met him at the door.

Most people called her Ellie, but the two of them had never been that friendly. He could see from the look on her face nothing had changed.

Her eyes blazed. "We don't allow tramps in this vicinity."

"I'm not a tramp, Mrs. Addington."

"How do you know my name?"

"Ma'am, the last time you acted like I was the shoe-shine boy. The time before you thought I was your neighbor's gardener."

"We've *met*?" she asked, her tone brimming with indignation.

"I'd like to speak to Ginny."

"She's not here. She's having a dress made for Joseph's baptism."

"Who's Joseph?"

"Your cousin, of course."

Caleb smiled. "So, you do remember me?"

She rolled her eyes. "It's coming back to me now."

"You're planning on visiting Magnolia?" he asked.

"You don't need to act like it's such a surprise. With my husband traveling year-round, I come at least once a month to see my grandchildren." Her lips tugged upward. "I'm very fond of James and Joseph."

Caleb recalled Josh saying he didn't think his mother liked children. That might have been true at one point, but not anymore. She adored three-year-old James and doted on the new baby just as much.

Her affection worked out well for Caleb because it meant that he got a glimpse of Ginny every so often.

She continued, "One day, I hope Ginny will have her own family. In fact, I've already bought a house for her."

Caleb felt like she'd dumped a pail of cold water over his head. She held him in her self-important gaze. Her lips pressed together, forming a thin line. "It's the red brick, over there."

She pointed over his shoulder. He didn't need to turn around and look. He already knew the house would be a lavish, fancy home, the type of home he could never offer his wife.

He kept his eyes on her. Her shoulders squared. Indignation poured from her as she gave him her coldest, haughtiest look. He didn't blink. He'd stared down worse than Eleanor Addington.

"I have plans for Ginny, too," he said quietly.

"I know," she hissed. "Your plans don't amount to much more than a dusty, cramped bunkhouse. You think that's fair to Ginny?"

"Mrs. Addington, I got a whole lot more to offer than that."

She sneered and folded her arms across her chest.

He tugged the letter from his pocket, keeping his eyes fixed on hers. She scowled, took the letter from him and read it. He watched as her eyes moved over the letter from the law firm in Austin. Her brow knit as she read the short letter. She shook her head as her anger grew, but when she lifted her eyes to his, she recovered her senses, composed herself and gave him a bland look.

"This changes nothing."

"I'm sorry ma'am. I hate to argue with a lady, but I think you know that it changes everything." He turned and went down the stairs. At the bottom, he put his Stetson on his head, glanced back and winked at her. "See you soon, Ellie."

The End (but there's more!)

Author's note: What follows is Caleb Bentley's story, the final story in the Bluebonnet Brides Series. It is a short story, not long enough to merit its own book, but it has loads of humor and love.

I didn't plan to write this story, but over the course of writing the five Bluebonnet Bride books, I came to have an affection for Caleb that I just could not ignore, and I had to tell his story. I hope you enjoy it.

Love's Destiny

The Final Story from the Bluebonnet Brides Series

Caleb and Ginny's Story

Charlotte Dearing

Chapter One

Ginny

Ginny frowned at the forged letter. Would she be able to pull the wool over Caleb's eyes? Maybe she should start over, she thought. But that would just introduce more problems. For one, she'd need to make sure no one, especially Sophia or Josh, would ever find the unused letter. There'd be no end to the questions if they did. And who's to say a new letter would be any better than this one. And, even though she felt very comfortable forging signatures, she still knew it was wrong, and she preferred not to forge any more signatures than absolutely necessary. Ginny smiled at her noble perspective.

She decided to stay the course. This letter was fine. Caleb couldn't possibly know what President Harrison's handwriting looked like. Caleb would be pleased and excited. His pride wouldn't allow suspicion or trickery to enter his hard, stubborn, exasperating head.

She gritted her teeth, but instantly regretted her tight grip on the pen. She'd clasped the pen too hard, making ink spill from the tip. Shiny, black pools of ink stained her paper and now she'd have to start all over anyway.

She groused, took out a fresh sheet of paper and started her fifth attempt. Ellie had given her a packet of fancy stationery when she turned sixteen. At the time, she couldn't have imagined using it for such an amusing purpose, a prank designed to get Caleb's attention.

Caleb Bentley might try to ignore her, but he wouldn't ignore the President.

She began her letter once again and this time her words flowed better. She wrote in what she hoped looked presidential, explaining that the White House wished to invite Mr. Caleb Bentley to work in the Presidential Stables. She added that everyone in Washington had heard of his skill with animals, and most especially horses. Could he come as soon as possible to take on the task of gentling his unruly Tennessee Walker?

Pausing at the end of her letter, she pondered how to sign the president's name. "Ben" seemed too informal. "Benjamin Harrison" might work. Did the President have a middle name? From her school studies she knew he was the grandson of William Harrison, the ninth president, but didn't recall much more. The man's name might not fit in the space she had. It was a dilemma. Finally, she decided on "President H."

After the ink dried, she folded the paper carefully and tucked the letter into an envelope. She hadn't thought to procure stamps and regretted that oversight. Without a stamp, her ruse would be discovered quickly. No matter. Even if Caleb believed that President Harrison had written him a letter for an instant, it would be worth the trouble.

She rose from her writing desk and moved to the window. Drawing the lace curtain back, she glimpsed Sophia and Josh returning from the orchard. Sophia carried her son, James, and Josh toted a basket brimming with plums. With a smile, Ginny turned away from the window.

She met Josh and Sophia at the back door of the kitchen. "Could I talk you into giving me a few of those plums?"

"You can have all of them," Sophia said. "I need to put James down for his afternoon nap."

"What do you plan to make?" Josh asked, setting the plums on the counter.

Ginny drew a deep breath and inhaled the perfume of the wine-red plums. They never had freshly picked fruit in Boston. Texas definitely had its joys. She cupped a plum in her hands, lifted it and admired the color and scent.

"I'll make a pie," she said. "And if Rosalinda doesn't chase me out of the kitchen, I might have time to make a plum streusel."

Josh and Sophia left her to bake, and she went straight to work. Rosalinda would return soon from wherever she was and commandeer the oven and stove. The further along she could get, the less she'd have to hear from Rosalinda.

Ginny kept watch for Caleb while she worked briskly, mixing up and rolling out pie dough. She washed, pitted and sliced the plums and stirred in sugar, flour, cinnamon and nutmeg. She arranged a pastry lattice over the filling and set it in the oven.

Before she started the streusel cake, she spied Caleb. He returned from the pastures. He was alone. Perfect. She went to her room and grabbed the letter, then returned to the kitchen window just in time to see him disappear into the barn. She hurried across the yard and followed him in. He was unsaddling his horse.

"Is this yours?" she asked, holding out the envelope. Her heart thundered inside her chest. A breathless laugh escaped her lips. She bit her tongue to keep from giving herself away.

He frowned, took it from her and opened it. His eyes widened. His lips parted as he drew a sharp breath. "Where'd you find this?"

Drat! She hadn't anticipated that question. "Well, let's see."

Turning the paper to show her, he stared in disbelief. "It's from the President of the United States. Look at this! He wants me to come to the White House and train his horse. Land sakes, wait till my father hears about this."

"What an amazing surprise."

His eyes lit with happiness. "It sure is. I don't know what sort of money the President pays for horse training. Want to know the first thing I'll buy?"

Ginny tried to keep from rolling her eyes. "A new cowboy hat, probably. Or a fancy saddle, I'll bet."

He shook his head. "I'm not going to buy a hat or a saddle."

"Some new chaps, fringed ones like Francisco's?"

He tucked the letter into his pocket and went back to untacking his horse. "Wrong again."

"I give up. Tell me."

He smiled, his white teeth flashing against his suntanned skin. "I'd buy something for a girl I'm sweet on."

She felt the blood slowly drain from her face. So that was why he ignored her. He had a sweetheart. Fury simmered inside her heart. She folded her arms across her chest. "Doesn't *that* sound peachy keen. What are you going to buy her?"

"I don't know," he drawled. "What strikes your fancy, Ginny?"

She blinked and waited for him to laugh or crack a joke. She'd written the letter to tease him, but now it seemed she might be the one getting teased.

He draped his arm over his horse's neck and gave her an appraising look. "I know you're just sixteen, but one day I'll buy you something pretty."

She hadn't expected the conversation to turn this direction. He seemed hardly impressed with the letter and more intent on telling her outlandish things. He never seemed to give her a second look and now he spoke of wanting to buy her gifts.

"Let me show you something," he said, taking a step away from his horse. "Come on, Dusty, show Ginny how you propose to a pretty filly."

The horse snorted and took a step back. To Ginny's amazement, the horse then stepped one foot forward, bent the other knee, and dipped his head. The horse looked as if he were dropping to one knee to offer a proposal. She laughed breathlessly, lifting a trembling hand to her lips.

"Atta way," Caleb said. "Up."

The horse obeyed promptly. For a long moment, neither Caleb nor Ginny said a word. Her heart thumped double-time as she tried to compose her wild thoughts. He'd never given her any sign he cared about her. If anything, he went out of his way to avoid her.

Rosalinda's voice pulled her from her confusion. The cook called from the back porch. "Ginny! Your pie!"

"Oh, dear," she murmured, turning on her heel. "I must go."

She hurried back to the house, raced into the kitchen and checked the pie. Rosalinda was nowhere to be seen, but probably wanted the oven for her own baking. Her hands shaking, Ginny hastily arranged the sliced plums in a baking dish. She mixed flour and sugar for the topping, sprinkled it over the fruit and tucked the streusel into the oven.

Her mind spun with turmoil. In the barn, Caleb Bentley spoke of being sweet on her. It was beyond comprehension.

She tidied the kitchen so Rosalinda wouldn't fuss about the mess. When she was done, she took the pie and streusel out of the oven and set them on the counter to cool. A movement in the barnyard caught her attention. Caleb strolled to the corral, a smile playing on his lips. He stopped to talk to Rosalinda's husband, Francisco, and showed him the letter. Ginny squeezed her eyes shut, cringing inwardly, wishing for the life of her she could take back her prank letter.

Chapter Two

Caleb

That afternoon, Caleb saddled up a troublesome mustang, a wild one that Josh had bought him a month ago. Along the way, someone had named the horse Brimstone. With a name like that, it went without saying the bronc would know a trick or two.

All the cowboys had heard the story of Caleb's letter by now. Some were very happy for Caleb, slapping him on the back and telling him he was, indeed, the best horse handler they'd ever seen. But a few men didn't respond the way Caleb thought they should.

One said he'd also received a letter, from Mrs. Harrison, asking him to come to Washington to help train their pet goat, Whiskers, to pull the children's carriage. And the cook made a comment that he'd been asked to come show the kitchen folks how to make chili and cornbread. For the life of him, Caleb wasn't quite sure why they joked about his letter. They were probably just jealous.

Caleb climbed into the saddle. Brimstone proceeded to pitch and buck. Caleb was certain all four hooves cleared the ground. The height more than impressed the cowpunchers gathered around the rails of the corral. They whooped and hollered, louder than usual, Caleb thought. Some called encouragement. Others offered advice. Caleb wasn't certain if they were cheering him or the horse.

Just when he thought he had the bronco under control, Brimstone launched so high off the ground that Caleb feared the horse might hurt himself.

Before he'd even gotten on the horse, he took off his spurs to keep from jabbing the gelding's flanks. He'd bridled the horse with a simple hackamore. Now he worried that Brimstone might get injured anyway. Caleb tried to turn the horse in a tight circle. It was a tactic that oftentimes kept horses from bucking. Brimstone wasn't having it.

As much as Caleb enjoyed giving the cowboys a good show, he didn't want the horse to lame himself. He needed to leave the corral. He'd head to the open pastures to give Brimstone room to stretch his legs. That would wear the rascal down.

"Gate," Caleb yelled.

Two cowboys hurried to the gate, unlatched it and let it swing open. Caleb reined the horse around to face the open gate. Brimstone didn't need a second invitation. He bolted for the opening. In four strides he reached the gate. The cowboys darted out of his way.

"Dang it," one of them yelped.

"Brimstone's faster 'an a greased spit!"

"He don't look like he's gonna stop."

As Caleb and the horse galloped past, he heard the cook yell. "That bronc ain't gonna stop till he gets clear to the White House!"

The men's laughter rang in his ears but soon faded. The mustang's hooves drummed on the path. Caleb bent low and loosened the reins. With each stride, the powerful mustang gained speed. Wind whipped through the horse's mane. Caleb's eyes watered. Pastures, trees and landscape blurred. A thrill of satisfaction rippled through Caleb as they thundered down the path.

His uncles and father didn't believe you should indulge a mustang's wild nature. They thought letting a horse run would only encourage the animal's bad behavior. Caleb didn't agree. Over the years, he'd found that plenty of rogue horses had too much fire in their blood. A good, hard run tempered a little of the fire without breaking the horse's spirit.

Not too far off in the distance, the river sparkled in the afternoon sunshine. They raced toward the water. The mustang's breath grew ragged. His glossy coat darkened with sweat. Caleb reined the horse the direction of a sandy bank. When they were a few paces from the water, the horse slowed to an easy lope and then to a trot. When he reached the water, he halted.

Caleb spoke gently. "Don't stop now, fraidy cat."

The horse took a few tentative steps into the stream and stopped. He lowered his head to the rippling water and snapped his lips on the surface. Caleb tugged his head up and coaxed him into a walk. "Nope, you're too hot to have a drink."

Caleb kept the horse in the center of the stream. The cool water would sooth Brimstone's pasterns and fetlocks. When they reached a deeper section, the water reached his hocks. Caleb would have liked to linger but the rascal might just drop into the cool water and roll. In the past, Caleb had ridden a few horses that decided a walk in the river was time for a soak.

Caleb didn't feel like getting doused, not today. Especially not with the President's letter in his pocket. He coaxed the horse out of the stream and turned for home. Brimstone's manners had improved considerably. He plodded along the path, alert but calm. When they returned to the barnyard, the cowboys had gone. Caleb untacked the horse and rubbed liniment on the mustang's legs.

His Uncle Josh entered the barn, a smile lighting his face. "Heard you and Brimstone put on one heck of a show."

"Yes, sir." Caleb pet the horse's neck. "I think some of the men hoped that Brimstone would pitch me off."

"What's this I hear about you getting a letter from Washington?"

Caleb felt his face heat with embarrassment. He hadn't meant to boast about it but couldn't resist telling his uncle's cowboys. The news had traveled quickly. He hoped his father didn't learn of the letter. Caleb wanted to tell his father himself.

He patted his trouser pocket. When he didn't find the letter, he searched his other pocket and his breast pocket too. "Dang," he muttered. Horror dawned on him. He'd lost the most important letter he'd ever received.

"It must have fallen out. In the corral. Or maybe the river."

Josh crossed his arms. "Where did you find this letter?"

"Ginny brought it to me. This morning. Here in the barn."

"Ginny, huh?" Josh's eyes sparked with amusement. "Ginny brought you a letter. From President Harrison."

For a moment, Caleb wondered why his uncle grinned at him, or why he'd posed the question about Ginny. Slowly he realized that Josh hadn't been asking, he'd been trying to tell him that the girl had tricked him. Again.

"That little brat," he growled. "I ought to toss her in the water trough by the corral. I ought to..."

His words faded as he tried to think of a fitting punishment for Ginny. Josh, usually so protective of Ginny, merely chuckled.

"I wouldn't really do anything like that to her," Caleb grumbled.

That night he ate supper at the house with Sophia, Josh and their baby James. He said nothing to Ginny but noted that she looked increasingly miserable throughout the dinner. After the meal, she brought out a plum pie, and served the group, offering him an extra-large slice.

"I'll be right back," she said. "I made some whipped cream for the pie."

She hurried out of the dining room. Sophia and Josh fussed over James, and while they were distracted, Caleb sprinkled a generous serving of salt over Ginny's slice. A moment later, she returned with the cream, served the group and took her seat.

Caleb took a bite. "This is delicious, Ginny."

She beamed at his words of praise. Everyone else agreed, but Caleb noted that it was his admiration that she awaited. She took a dainty bite of her pie, chewed slowly. Her eyes widened with alarm. Her face pinked.

"What's the matter, Ginny?" he said under his breath. He pushed the salt shaker her direction. "Maybe it needs a little *salt*?"

She shook her head. "Caleb Bentley. You are the most low-down scoundrel I've ever known. You ruined my plum pie."

"Just one piece." He chuckled. "Mine's perfectly fine."

She let out a huff.

"I'm not finished with you yet," he muttered. "Not by a long shot."

Chapter Three

Ginny

Fortunately, sweet Caleb Bentley never once carried through with any sort of retribution. Thank goodness, too. From that moment forward, the two of them enjoyed a tentative peace. He was always cordial, never going out of his way to ignore her, and she refrained from pranks, never forging another letter from a President.

The following spring when she visited Ellie in Houston, she found herself thinking about Caleb more and more. She didn't dare confess her feelings to Ellie. Josh's mother didn't care for him. She seemed determined to marry Ginny off to a wealthy banker-type in Houston.

When she returned to Magnolia, Josh met her at the train station. He always seemed grateful to Ginny that she visited his mother. They chatted on the way back, discussing sundry topics. Ginny tamped down her curiosity about Caleb. Was he at the ranch? She never knew if he might be working for Josh or one of the other Bentley men.

As they drew close to Josh's ranch, she spied a movement on the side of the road. "Stop the wagon, Josh. I think I see something."

Josh sighed, drew back on the reins and brought the wagon to a halt. Without waiting for his help, she clambered down. A dog, a puppy from the looks of things, lay in the sodden grass. Josh came to her side and crouched over the animal.

The small pup lay unmoving, his fur matted and filthy.

"Ginny, I think he's gone."

She reached down and stroked its head. To her surprise, the pup whimpered. Josh muttered a few words of dismay. Ginny could tell he didn't care for her touching the dog. He probably imagined it might be vicious, but the little fellow was small, painfully thin and no threat to anyone.

Unable to resist the pitiful sight, she tugged the silk shawl from her shoulders, wrapped it around the dog and drew him into her arms.

"Is Caleb at the ranch?" She hoped her tone sounded casual.

Josh grumbled and helped her back to the wagon. "He's there all right. He stuck around this week. Wonder why?"

Ginny might have smiled at his words, if her heart hadn't hurt for the small, suffering pup. For the rest of the trip to the ranch, she held him close, trying to warm him. Her shawl and dress grew damp from the pup's drenched fur. Wouldn't Ellie Addington have a fit if she saw the state of Ginny's newest dress?

Caleb met the wagon when they arrived. A smile lit his face, one that warmed Ginny's heart. His smile turned to a frown when he saw that she held a small, wet bundle in her arms. He helped her down, skipped any preliminaries, and tugged the shawl away from the pup's head.

"I'll just take care of the wagon," Josh grumbled.

"I found this little fellow on the side of the road," Ginny said. "I hoped you might be able to help him."

"Hey there, little fella," Caleb said softly.

"Don't mind me," Josh added, a little louder. "I can unload her trunks. It's no trouble at all."

Caleb looked up. "Thanks, Uncle Josh." He took the pup from Ginny. "Let's see if we can warm this scrawny fella up."

Over the course of the afternoon, Ginny helped Caleb tend to the forlorn pup. They worked in the gardening shed next to the orchard. After they dried him off, they let him wander around the small shed. The pup was nothing more than skin and bones, but he was uninjured.

Rosalinda brought a small dish of food, rice mixed with small bits of chicken. Ginny saw another side of Josh's cook as the woman knelt beside the dog. Rosalinda hid her warm heart most of the time. As she patted the little pup, she murmured softly in Spanish.

"Good thing you found the little dog, Ginny," she said before returning to the house. "You should name him Lucky."

Caleb grinned at Ginny. "Lucky's a good name. But he won't be a little dog for long."

"Not with Rosalinda cooking for him," Ginny laughed.

"Not only that, look at the size of those paws."

Lucky yawned, crossed the shed and sniffed Ginny's silken scarf she'd dropped by the corner. He pawed it, circled a few times, flopped down and promptly fell fast asleep, his nose tucked under his tail.

Chapter Four

One year later...

Caleb

Caleb had driven cattle to the Fort Worth stockyard plenty of times before, but this was the first time he arrived with his own, personal herd. A little better than a hundred head. They kicked up dust and grit along with a tremendous ruckus as they entered the main holding pen.

The stockyard's head wrangler looked them over and grinned at Caleb. Over the course of the next hour, the cattle were counted, the steers culled, leaving the cows with their calves. The calves and the grown cattle bawled and caterwauled. Caleb trotted around the pen to the chuck wagon.

Despite the racket, Lucky slept in the back of the wagon. The dog was fully grown and just as Caleb had suspected, turned out to be a good-sized dog. Caleb dismounted and hitched his horse to the railing.

Frank, the cook, glanced over his shoulder. "You going out with us tonight, boss?"

Caleb took off his hat and wiped the sweat from his brow. "Nope."

"How come you never want to have any fun, preacher boy?"

"I'm not interested in that kind of fun." He summoned the dog. Lucky rose, yawned loudly and hopped down from the wagon. Caleb turned his attention to his cook. "Frank?"

"Yeah?"

"That's the last time you call me preacher boy."

Frank's jaw dropped and he recoiled. "Why, I've known you since you was knee-high to-"

"Don't matter."

Caleb waited, keeping his gaze fixed on the older man.

"Well... dang, all right then. Fine."

"Something else, Frank. You got a wife and family back in Magnolia. If you want to work for me again, you won't spend the evening tom-cattin' around Fort Worth. Got me?"

Caleb watched as the old-timer went from dismay to anger and finally stunned disbelief. If Frank were smart, he'd abide by Caleb's words. At the beginning of the drive, Caleb told his men that he'd give each a bonus for a successful drive. By that he meant completing the journey without losing any of the herd. All his men, a half-dozen cowboys, waited for the official count from the wrangler. While each of them would go home with a bonus, not all would get invited on the next cattle drive.

After a long moment, Frank looked away. "I got you, sir."

Caleb nodded and crossed the busy stockyard. He moved through the maze of accounting offices, his spurs ringing with each step. Lucky trotted behind him. He found the clerk's counter, received his payment and the good news that they hadn't lost a single head.

As he left the crowded office, Caleb did some quick sums. His small savings account disheartened him at times. It seemed he'd never have enough. His only goal was to save for a parcel of land to call his own. When he owned property, he could offer for Ginny. Not before. The drive had been a success, but he was still a long way from what he needed to buy his own place.

Countless times his father had offered to simply give him a stretch of land. Caleb couldn't bring himself to accept a handout. He loved and respected his father, but years ago when he discovered that Thomas wasn't truly his father, he lost a part of himself. If he wasn't really a Bentley, he didn't know who he was. But he did know that he didn't want charity.

That night, when Caleb checked into his hotel, he ordered dinner to be brought up. He ate alone in his room with only Lucky for company. The dog sat beside the table, his big brown eyes following each bite of meat that Caleb ate.

"All right, ya big dummy. I saved you the bone and left plenty for you to gnaw off."

Caleb gave him the bone along with a few chunks of potato. The dog thumped his tail with gratitude. Caleb moved to the window and looked out on the sights of Cowtown. From the third floor of the hotel he could see as far as the distant railroad line. The iron rails glinted in the last rays of sunset.

The night before he left Magnolia, he heard Sophia talking about Ginny. She told Josh that the girl would go with Ellie to Fort Worth to attend a fancy dinner party. The dinner would be held in the home of a man who owned several cottonseed mills.

The success of the cattle drive pleased him, but that satisfaction faded as he thought of Ginny somewhere out there, without him, at some fancy dinner party. Some other man might tempt Ginny with glittering promises.

His heart thudded painfully. He stared out the window. The first few stars flickered in the distance as the sky darkened. Caleb remained, unwilling to turn away, and watched dusk give way to nightfall.

Chapter Five

Ginny

At first, Ginny had regarded Ellie's invitations with mixed feelings. She enjoyed the new sights and had to admit she relished the way Josh's mother spoiled her. Never had she imagined owning so many fine things. No matter how much she protested, Ellie insisted on new frocks, fancy hats, and boots she had specially cobbled to compensate for Ginny's injured leg.

The best part of traveling was returning to Magnolia. Caleb's sweet, bashful smile warmed her heart a little more each time.

Ellie was not fond of Caleb, to put it mildly, and Ginny wondered if part of the reason was that Ellie was not very happy in her own marriage. She was married to a man named Niles, an investor and owner of mines who was rarely home. Ellie never mentioned Niles, so Ginny really had no cause to think Ellie was unhappy, but it helped her deal with Ellie's poor treatment of Caleb to think Niles must be a horrible husband.

Just before her eighteenth birthday, she received a letter from Ellie, saying that Niles would be in Virginia for several months, and inviting her on a trip to San Francisco.

This time, when she packed her bags, she couldn't help being wistful. When she attended dinners and soirees with

Ellie, she was certain that young men gave her lingering looks of admiration. She didn't care for any of that. What she yearned for most of all was for Caleb to regard her with something more than courtesy.

The morning she was to leave, Josh told her that Caleb would take her to the train station. Her heartbeat quickened at the sound of his name. Part of her wanted him to ask her to stay, to give her a reason to stay.

He arrived late morning, dressed in his Sunday best, looking grim. She wondered if he resented having to set aside his tasks. In her foolish imaginings, she'd conjured up the notion he'd asked to take her to the station, but it was clear from his frown, he only took her as a favor to Josh. He loaded her trunks and helped her to the wagon. They drove to Magnolia under darkening skies.

"Looks like rain," she offered.

"It does."

"Josh says we could use some rain."

"We could."

Ginny sighed, wishing she could find a way to break past his stoic reticence. "You ever think about offering for a girl?"

Caleb started, jerking his head around to face her. "That's a heck of a question, isn't it?"

"You think I'm being forward?"

"I do."

"I never suggested I wanted you to offer for me. I simply asked if you considered the notion. I believe plenty of young men start to think about a wife and family at some point."

"I know that. I plan to offer for a girl. Just not yet."

"Why not?"

"I don't have anything to offer a wife. Yet."

"If she loved you, she wouldn't need very much. She'd be just happy to be by your side."

"Is that so?"

Caleb seemed to be getting madder with every mile.

Maybe she was too. "You got a girl in mind, Caleb Bentley?"

"I do, in fact."

Now Ginny was furious. Sitting beside him, she curled her gloved hands into tight fists and fumed. "Maybe she's not good enough for you, if you're so darned worried she wants you to provide all sorts of fine things."

"Maybe she's just too sassy for her own good. And that's why she keeps on running off hither and yon. She might be too proud to be content in a little town like Magnolia."

Ginny squeezed her eyes shut. Whenever she let her temper get away from her, tears were soon to follow. She was determined not to suffer the humiliation of crying in front of a beast like Caleb Bentley. Her ire soon faded, but she still did not trust herself to speak.

They traveled the rest of the way in silence. When they arrived, Caleb helped her down, carried her trunk to the platform and left without a word. Ginny watched him as he walked away. Her breath caught in her throat. Once more, tears threatened.

To her relief, he returned after hitching the team. He waited a few paces from her. He probably lingered because cowpunchers and drifters and sundry types began to arrive and Josh wouldn't want her to be bothered by the rough men.

"I don't need a chaperone," she snapped. "Ellie's coming on the train."

He gave her a bemused smile, which only annoyed her once again. The train whistle pierced the air. In the distance, smoke plumed. The crowd gathered. Men shook hands and said good-bye. A handful of women kissed their men. The locomotive thundered around the bend, wheels screeching, the conductor waving from the window.

Porters jumped from the train as it rolled to a stop. The brakes hissed. Steam billowed.

Caleb instructed the porters to load her trunk. She nodded to him and turned to board, but he caught her elbow and drew her back. He trailed his hand down her arm and clasped her hand in his. She drew a sharp breath of surprise.

"Come back to me, Ginny."

A wave of confusion came over her. "Right now?"

He shook his head. "Not now. Always."

Someone called her name over the crowd. Ellie stood on the train and waved to her. The train whistle blasted. Caleb ushered her onto the train, his hand on the small of her back as he shielded her from the passengers jostling for position.

Before she ascended the stairs, he tugged her elbow. "Promise me, Ginny."

Stunned by his words, she somehow managed a response. "I promise you."

She boarded the train and followed Ellie to their compartment. As Ellie spoke with the porter, Ginny stood by the window, her gaze fixed on Caleb as the train lurched. The whistle blew and it gathered momentum. Caleb lifted his fingers to his lips and kissed them, then handed the kiss to the air between them, as if a butterfly were lifting off his fingers, ready to fly to her. The train rounded the bend. She watched until he disappeared from her view.

Ellie came to the window and gave a sigh. Ginny was certain she'd have something unflattering to say about Caleb. Ellie had always made it clear she didn't think much of him.

"Such a nice boy," she said.

"I thought you didn't care for him."

Ellie's brows lifted. Her lips parted with surprise. "Au contraire. I think it's precious how he's always had a tender heart. He feels sorry for any stray soul."

Ginny searched Ellie's face for a sign that she spoke in jest. Ellie offered a sunny smile.

"You mean animals?" Ginny asked.

"Of course, I mean animals. What did you think I meant?" Ellie gasped softly. "Did you think I meant he felt sorry for *people*? Oh, Ginny, darling, I'm sure that's not why Calvin fixed your boots so long ago. I'm sure that wasn't out of sympathy for you, silly girl. Shall we have tea? I ordered your favorite tarts. The lemon curd."

Chapter Six

Caleb

At times, Caleb's other uncles groused about how much he worked for his Uncle Josh. He had no trouble justifying the time he spent working for Josh. He paid him very well. Caleb was a businessman, he explained to them. He'd work for whoever paid him the most.

Lately that was Josh.

His duties ranged from riding the new fence lines to check that the barbed wire hadn't been cut, to teaching young James how to ride. This afternoon, he gave James a riding lesson. The boy rode Cinders, a horse that had to be the oldest mount in all of Magnolia.

"Show me how you get ol' Cinders to halt." Caleb stood in the middle of the corral, holding a lead line attached to the mare's bridle.

James tugged the reins back. Cinders took a few more steps and came to a stop.

"What do you tell her?" Caleb reminded gently.

"Good girl." James patted the mare's neck.

Caleb smiled. "Before that."

James frowned. "Whoa?"

"That's all right. Next time, buckaroo, give her a little heads-up and tell her whoa." He gathered the line, looping it as he crossed the corral. "You're getting better every day."

Sophia came to the corral, Joseph on her hip. "Look at my big, grown-up boy."

Sophia hadn't wanted James to learn how to ride just yet. She thought he was far too young, but the fact of the matter was that all the Bentley boys learned to ride early. Caleb couldn't ever recall a time when he *didn't* know how to ride. His father had probably put him on a pony right around the time Caleb had learned to walk. Maybe before.

"Let's untack the mare here in the corral," Caleb told James. "That way she can take a roll. Scratch her back and kick up her heels."

James's eyes lit with laughter. "That's so funny. Silly Cinders."

"I'm half-amazed the old girl can get back up," Caleb said under his breath.

Sophia smiled, reached through the rails and pet the mare's muzzle. "Don't insult my favorite horse, Caleb Bentley."

Caleb and James worked together to untack the horse. Caleb swung the boy into his arms so he could undo the cinch. Next, they took off her bridle. The mare turned away, strolled around the corral, her nose down. She circled and stopped in the middle. When she snorted and pawed the sand, James chuckled.

"Here we go," Caleb said in a croaking tone to imitate the voice of an old person. It always earned him a laugh from both children.

Cinder's knees bent. Her back legs buckled. Slowly, with what looked like infinite care, she eased lower, inching towards the sand.

"It's gonna be any day now," Caleb rasped.

The mare sank to the ground and began to roll. After several attempts, she made it over to the other side. Caleb and the boys clapped softly. With a groan, she heaved herself to her feet and shook.

"The mare's got some life in her yet," Caleb remarked.

"I wanted to thank you for teaching James," Sophia said. "He's over the moon about his riding lessons."

"Happy to do it," Caleb said.

James wandered away from the corral to pet a farmyard cat that dozed in the sunshine. Joseph squirmed in Sophia's arms, and she set him down so he could join his brother. The boys stroked the cat's fur. She got up and circled them, rubbing against their shins. The boys were always gentle with the ranch animals, Caleb noted with approval. Even Joseph, who didn't even speak yet.

"You seem to be in good spirits," Sophia remarked. "I thought you might miss Ginny. She's been gone almost a month."

"I got a letter from her today," Caleb said.

"Really?" She pressed her lips into a tight line. "That's nice. She never writes me."

"She never writes me either." He pulled the letter from his pocket. "Would you like to read it?"

She took the letter and read it, her eyes widening. Caleb chuckled.

"Why are you smiling?" Sophia demanded. "She says she doesn't really care for you and that you shouldn't wait for her."

"Don't forget the part about me marrying a Magnolia girl. That she's too good for the likes of me."

Sophia handed him the letter back. "Ginny would never say something like that. I'm sure of it."

"Ginny didn't write the letter."

Sophia closed her eyes and rubbed her forehead. "Eleanor Addington's up to her tricks."

He tucked the letter back into his pocket. "At least she didn't call me Carlos this time."

Chapter Seven

Ginny

Ellie Addington enjoyed the social life. She especially loved garden parties held in the springtime. Over the years, Ginny had attended scores of them with Ellie, but none so lovely as the party held each year at the home of the Hollister family. A few months after returning from California, Ginny accompanied Ellie on another trip. It took some time to reach the Hollister home near the Louisiana border. The party was the high point of the garden party season.

Ginny and Ellie strolled the gardens, admiring the profusion of azalea blooms. Ellie waved a young man over and chatted with him as they meandered along the wandering paths. Ginny attended to Ellie's conversation, or tried, but her mind drifted to thoughts of Caleb Bentley.

She wondered what Caleb was doing that very moment. She felt her lips tug up as she pictured him in his boots and chaps. When she first met him, he'd been a slim young man of eighteen. Since then, his physique had changed. Hewn by hard work, his shoulders broadened, his arms strengthened. His build had grown more powerful.

"Isn't that right, Ginny?"

She blinked at Ellie, trying desperately to recall what the woman had just said. "Pardon me?"

Ellie gave her an indulgent smile and turned back to the young man she'd been speaking to. "Sweet Ginny gets distracted when you're around."

The young man, Edmund something or other, blushed as he turned his admiring gaze to Ginny.

"You get distracted, do you?" he asked, an optimistic shine in his eyes.

Ginny searched for a polite response. She recalled meeting the young man once before, but beyond that had little memory of him. He was nothing more than an acquaintance at best.

"Of course, she does," Ellie replied. "I was just telling Edmund about how perilous life in the wilds of Texas is, Ginny dear. Why, just the stories that the O'Brian girls tell would be enough to give a sensible girl pause."

Ginny smiled, relieved to change the subject. "It's true. They had their share of adventure on their way to Texas. They were all mail-order brides from Boston. Grace came first, only to find the man she'd married by proxy had passed away."

Ellie waved a gloved hand. "Pooh! She makes it sound like he met his reward during a Sunday nap. The man was killed by a rattlesnake."

Edmund grimaced as a gnat buzzed past. It flew away, but returned, this time landing on the broad expanse of his forehead. He yelped, jumped from foot to foot as he batted his hands in the air. When it flew off, he drew a deep sigh and tugged his coat down. "I've heard of those. Gracious, I'm glad they don't have any in the better parts of a respectable city."

"That's right," Ellie said, giving Ginny a pointed look before going on. "Poor Grace was strong-armed into marriage just like her sister, Faith, who came to Texas a few months later."

Ellie liked to recount the tales of Magnolia at every garden party. It was her way of showing Ginny how ghastly life in

Magnolia could be. It was also her way to give young, eligible bachelors a slight nudge to offer for Ginny.

"You forgot to mention the bank robber." Ginny turned to Edmund. "It's the best part of the story, really."

"That's right!" Ellie set her gloved hand on Edmund's arm. "On the way to Magnolia, Faith was beset by a dangerous bank robber and forced to deliver a bag of stolen loot to Magnolia. Her husband-to-be, the sheriff, threatened to throw her in jail and throw away the key."

Edmund's jaw dropped a quarter inch.

Ginny smiled at his consternation. "They're blissfully married now."

Ellie waved off her words with a dismissive flick of her wrist. "Let me tell you about the worst Bentley of the bunch." She lowered her voice for dramatic effect. "Luke Bentley."

"What did he do?" Edmund frowned. "I'm almost afraid to ask."

"When the youngest O'Brian, Hope, refused his proposal," Ellie recounted, "the rogue traveled to Boston and forced her to marry him."

Ginny shook her head. "Remember? First, he burned her bookshop down, made certain she was evicted from her boarding house and *then* forced her to marry him."

Ellie rolled her eyes. "The details about the bookshop burning are a little unclear, but if you met Luke Bentley, you'd know he was the culprit. He just has the air of a..."

Ellie let her words fade but gave him a solemn look to convey just what she meant.

Ginny sighed. "Scoundrel."

"My stories are better when Ginny's not here to embellish the details." Ellie gave Edmund a sparkling smile. "How many banks does your father own now? I've lost count."

Edmund flushed. "Well, Mrs. Addington, I'm afraid that's a bit of a painful subject."

"Painful?" Ellie snapped. "For whom?"

Ginny watched as Edmund's color deepened to a mottled crimson. Sympathy tugged at her heart.

He tugged at his collar. "My father, you see, decided to sell his banks."

Ellie recovered her composure. "Ah, well, I have to imagine he made a pretty penny. What will he do next? Invest in railways?"

Edmund grimaced. "No, ma'am."

"Shipping?" Ellie's voice held a hint of panic.

"My parents intend to donate most of the money to help build a hospital. For the poor."

Ellie paled. She set her hand on her chest. "What will you do?"

Edmund looked melancholy. "I'm not sure. My father suggested I get..." His words drifted off. His gaze sank downward. His shoulders slumped.

"He suggested what?" Ellie demanded.

Edmund swallowed hard, his Adam's apple bobbing up and down the length of his pale throat. He shuddered and looked Ellie in the eye and drew a slow, deep breath. "My father suggested that I learn a trade."

"Merciful heavens," Ellie whispered.

Ginny stared, trying to imagine Edmund working as a blacksmith or carpenter or, Lord forbid, a cattleman. It was impossible to picture the young man earning a livelihood by the sweat of his brow.

"I'm not sure what's gotten into papa," Edmund said. "Perhaps he's angry with me."

"Edmund," Ellie said, her voice shrill. "It sounds very much like he's angry with you. I'd endeavor to get back into his good graces." She set her hand on her heart and drew several deep breaths, trying to compose herself. After a moment, she turned her attention to the fountains near the gazebo. "Oh, look! The Tobins have arrived! Come, Ginny! Let's say hello, shall we?"

Chapter Eight

Caleb

Things changed suddenly for Caleb. He now owned land, and quite a lot of it.

Earlier that morning, he had signed the necessary papers to take over the deed. Caleb felt sure his parents would arrive soon after. He would have bet his bottom dollar, and sure enough, his father and Faith drove down the road in the buckboard. Standing on the top step of his new home, he waved.

Thomas stopped the buckboard in front of the house and set the brake.

"Where's the rest of the family?" Caleb asked.

"We left them with their Aunt Grace," his father said. After he helped Faith down, he grinned at Caleb and eyed the house. Faith stood beside him, a basket in her hand and studied the house as well.

"Not too bad, son," Thomas said. "Not bad at all."

"What a lovely home!" Faith exclaimed.

"You know I always intended to make my own way," Caleb said.

Thomas shook his head. "Just because you inherit property doesn't mean you got a handout, son. I been trying to tell you that for years."

"It's never right to expect anything from anybody," Caleb said. "I didn't think my mother's parents would name me in their will. I certainly didn't expect them to leave me their ranch. They always groused about my being a Bentley."

"You *are* a Bentley," Thomas said, his eyes darkening.

"Granddad always wanted me to take his name. When I refused, he said he was done with me."

"Son of a gun," Thomas growled.

Faith nudged him with her elbow. "Now, Thomas. Let's not speak ill of the departed."

His father grumbled a few inaudible words as he took Faith's arm and led her up the front steps. "Let's have the tour. It's been years since I stepped foot inside the old Montgomery place."

Caleb opened the front door and ushered Faith past. "It's the Bentley place now."

His father chuckled and patted Caleb's shoulder as he went inside. Caleb showed them the parlor, the kitchen and the dining room. His heart swelled with pride.

"After Granddad passed away, I came to visit Grandma as often as possible, so I could help her with things. As she got older, she got a bit of a soft spot in her heart for me. Still, I assumed she'd leave her property to some other kin. After her funeral last winter, I didn't think too much about what might happen. Bit of a surprise to get word from the lawyers in Austin."

"Sounds like a good surprise," his father said. "I'm glad she did the right thing."

Faith's eyes shone. "It warms my heart to think of my boy having a place of his own, and maybe even a wife soon?"

A flush came over him. Faith was the one person who still referred to him as a boy, but she always called him "her boy," which made it all right. When Ginny had first come to Magnolia, he'd told Faith that he intended to marry Ginny one day. Over the years, he'd confided in Faith, telling her the details of his feelings for the girl. From the beginning he'd yearned for Ginny's affection and prayed she might one day accept his proposal. Now the day drew near. His heartbeat quickened at the notion of asking for her hand.

"I intend to propose at Joseph's baptism next week. If Ellie Addington doesn't lock me in the root cellar."

"Let her just try." Faith pressed her lips together. "I won't let her come between you and Ginny anymore. It's time for her to step aside and let you two have the happiness you deserve."

Caleb smiled at her fierce words. "I know I can count on you to stick up for me, Momma Bear."

Her expression softened. She slipped her arm around his waist and gave him a hug. From the first time Faith had told him the story of Goldilocks and the Three Bears, years ago, Caleb had given her the nickname, Momma Bear. It was a joke they shared. She was as close to a mother as he'd ever known, and the name held. In the privacy of their home, he'd called her the term of endearment ever since.

The second story of the house was a single, large room with a window on each wall.

"A German fella owned the house before Granddad," Caleb said. "They had a passel of kids and the boys slept up here. The girls shared a room downstairs."

His father wandered to a window and looked out. "How many acres do you have? Around seven hundred, right?"

"Seven hundred and fifty," Caleb said. "With the money I've saved, I aim to buy more land."

They returned to the kitchen and Faith unpacked the lunch she'd brought. "I made your favorite, Dublin Coddle. And for dessert, there are oatmeal cookies and jam thumbprints."

Caleb felt like a kid before Christmas, almost too wound up to eat, but when Faith began to set the food out, his appetite came back in a hurry. Unable to wait, he reached for a cookie. Faith shook her head, but her lips quirked with amusement.

Chapter Nine

Ginny

A few days after the garden party, Ellie and Ginny set out for Magnolia. Ellie's criticism of Caleb grew harsher the closer they got to Magnolia. The journey seemed unending. Ellie talked about Caleb incessantly. She presented him in a poor light, maligned him. A time or two she'd flat-out lied.

They rode in Ellie's carriage past the outskirts of Magnolia through a heavy rainstorm. Despite the ghastly weather and Ellie's barbed words, Ginny's heart fluttered with excitement. Soon she'd see Caleb. She'd been counting the days.

Ellie droned on and on. "I saved the best for last." Her eyes glittered. "Caleb Bentley is not the son of Thomas Bentley."

Ginny's anger flared. Caleb had told her the story, perhaps a year or two ago. Caleb's mother had been in the family way when she married Thomas Bentley. After the wedding, she confessed the baby belonged to another man. Ginny knew the details, but it infuriated her that Ellie bandied about something so private and so painful.

"It's none of your concern, Ellie," Ginny said. "It's *nobody's* business."

Ellie stared. Her mouth dropped open.

Ginny might have laughed at the sight if she hadn't been overcome with a rush of indignation. This was likely the first time Eleanor Addington had ever been rendered speechless.

"Speaking poorly of him only reflects badly on you."

Ellie squeaked with indignation. "That boy doesn't even know who his father is."

"You might recall that I'm an orphan." Ginny spoke from between clenched teeth. "I don't know who my father is either."

She directed her attention out the rain-streaked window. The storm seemed to grow fiercer with each passing mile. Thank goodness they were near Sophia and Josh's ranch. Ellie was likely furious, and shocked too. Ginny had never spoken to her in that way before. Ellie probably chafed at Ginny's tone. Let her seethe, Ginny thought. It would serve her right.

They rode in silence. Rain drummed on the roof.

A short while later, the carriage stopped. Ginny could make out the driver's voice as he shouted. Perhaps there was a problem with one of the horses, or the carriage? She peered out the window once more. To her astonishment the river that ran near the Bentley ranch had overflowed its banks.

"He'll need to go further upstream," Ginny said, more to herself than anything.

Ellie gave a slight shake of her head. "Neville knows what he's doing, dear."

To Ginny's surprise, Ellie didn't sound put out. She sounded tired. Ginny studied the way her shoulders slumped, and her lips tugged downward. Ellie usually sat ramrod straight. Ginny felt sorry for Ellie. The older woman was often lonely and tried to fill her life with parties and endless travel to avoid being alone. When Ginny got married, Ellie would lose her traveling companion.

The carriage started moving. Ginny couldn't tell if the driver was proceeding upriver or if he intended to cross it here. Over the din of rainfall, she heard more shouting.

"Who is he shouting at?" Ginny asked.

"Some fool cowboy," Ellie muttered.

Some fool cowboy...

"Merciful heavens," Ginny whispered. She let out a small cry of dismay. "It must be Caleb."

Ellie scoffed. "If the shoe fits."

"He's trying to warn us off. He's telling the driver not to cross."

"Don't be so theatrical, dear. Neville was driving carriages before Caleb's slatternly mother brought him into the world."

Ginny recoiled at the cruel words. She turned away from Ellie, not trusting herself to reply.

The rain fell so heavily now that Ginny couldn't tell where they were. The driver's shouts were drowned out by the din. A horse whinnied in terror. Water seeped under the door of the carriage. At first it was no more than a trickle, but in a matter of seconds water rushed in, covering the floor.

"What on earth?" Ellie snapped.

They exchanged horrified looks. In the next instant, the door burst open. Before Ginny could cry out, water filled the carriage. The force of the water sent her tumbling out the door on the other side. She sank into the swirling depths. Arms flailing, she managed to swim to the surface. She gasped for air. The water pulled her under again.

When she came up a second time, a tree limb struck her shoulder. Pain shot down her arm. Despite the pain, she managed to grab the limb. Holding the branch kept her afloat. The current was strong and fast. She thought she saw the horses emerge from the river, some distance upstream. They pulled what was left of the carriage.

A cowboy that Ginny didn't recognize rode his horse down the riverbank. He swung his lasso over his head. Ellie flailed in the water, near the shore.

Ellie shouted at the cowboy. "Get the girl." She sputtered and coughed. The cowboy threw his lasso but Ginny lost sight of Ellie. She heard Ellie's voice again. "No! Get Ginny first."

Ginny's hands slipped on the slick wood. The leaden weight of her dress and petticoats pulled her deeper into the swirling torrent. Her fingers felt numb. Her palms raw. She slipped further. Closing her eyes, she prayed for strength. In the next moment, strong arms encircled her waist.

Caleb's gruff voice sounded next to her ear. "I got you, Ginny. You're safe. You're mine now."

Chapter Ten

Three Weeks Later...

Caleb

Piano music filled the small chapel. Caleb had never felt so jumpy. This was the day he'd dreamed of, and yet, he worried that at the last moment, Ginny might change her mind. Maybe Ellie would convince her she should marry a better man. He scanned the church and found Ellie, sitting in the front row, her eyes misting. That had to be a good sign. She'd come to the church, at least.

Hopefully she hadn't come so she could object to the wedding.

Caleb's father, his best man, patted his shoulder and offered a few encouraging words. His uncles, Matt and Luke, stood on the other side of his father, both of them smiling broadly at him, probably relishing his nervousness.

The doors opened. Josh ushered Ginny into the chapel. Caleb's breath caught in his lungs. Ginny looked radiant. He wondered if he were dreaming. A collective gasp rippled through the guests. Someone, probably Ellie, sobbed.

Ginny wore a lace gown. Faith and her two sisters had sewn the lace themselves. The three women had worked night and day for the last three weeks to have the dress completed in time. In addition to the lavish dress, she wore a veil.

Josh walked her down the aisle, stopped at the end, and lifted her veil. He gave her a kiss on the cheek, clapped Caleb on the shoulder, and then made his way to the first pew between his mother and Sophia. Caleb took Ginny's hands and held her gaze as the minister said the vows.

Her eyes shone with excitement. He felt his heart hammer. His blood rushed in his ears as time seemed to slow. His gaze drifted to her lips. In a moment he'd claim her with a kiss and make her his for the rest of his days.

Caleb was only half-aware of the minister's words. Suddenly they sounded a mite louder than they had a few moments before.

If any of you has a reason why these two should not be married, speak now or forever hold your peace...

Ginny's eyes widened. Her mouth curved into a tender smile as they waited. Silence followed. Finally, the minister continued. Ginny let out a breath. Caleb winked at her. They exchanged rings and when the minister pronounced them man and wife, Caleb lowered to brush a chaste kiss across her lips.

He led her out of the church and into a small courtyard.

"That was my first kiss," she whispered.

"Better be," he growled. "It was my first kiss, too."

She blushed. "Really?"

He gathered her in his arms, pulling her close. "What? You think I been running around kissing girls?"

She nodded. "I did, in fact, wonder."

He shook his head. "I've only ever wanted you, Ginny. Nobody else."

Caleb led her to a waiting buckboard, one that had been decorated with flowers and ribbons. He helped her up and took the seat beside her. The crowd gathered around the wagon. Children tossed flower petals.

Ellie eyed the buckboard and pressed her lips together.

Caleb braced himself for some sort of unkind word.

Josh came to Ellie's side and tucked her hand in the crook of his arm. "That's the way we do things in Magnolia."

"I know," Ellie replied. "At least the groom shaved his scruffy beard."

Caleb chuckled as he gathered the reins in his hands.

Ellie sniffed. "Half the time he looks like he just stepped out of a wanted poster."

"Ellie, one day I'll win you over," Caleb said.

To his surprise, she smiled at him. "You won me over when you pulled Ginny from the flooded river."

Faith and Sophia both nodded as did several other wedding guests.

Caleb marveled at her words. "I think she just said something nice to me."

The crowd dispersed, getting in their buggies and wagons and followed Caleb to Thomas's home, the old Bentley homestead. Mrs. Patchwell and Rosalinda had spent the day cooking and preparing for the wedding reception. The party was held in the garden. The sun shone, casting dappled sunlight across the tables and chairs. An enormous cake stood on a table in the center of the festivities.

Caleb and Ginny strolled hand-in-hand amongst their guests until it was time to eat. They gathered in a great circle and bowed their heads as Thomas said a blessing over the meal. After he finished, they said amen.

Ellie waved her hand. "I'd like to add a few words of thanksgiving. I'm so grateful for this family. Today is a special day and I'm thankful to be part of the celebration. I'm thankful for Caleb." Her eyes shone. She paused and swallowed before going on. "I hope that the Lord blesses you with many children and many happy years together."

"I'll be," Josh muttered.

Ellie went on. "Since Josh and Sophia seem determined to only have boys, I'd like to suggest a name for your daughter, if you're blessed with a girl child."

"I wonder what name she might conjure up," Luke muttered.

"Eleanor Bentley," Ellie said. "I don't think you could have a nicer name than that."

Caleb chuckled, went to Ellie and embraced her. Ginny hugged her as well.

And then the entire Bentley family gathered together to break bread.

Chapter Eleven

Two Years Later...

Ellie

As the sun lifted over the horizon, Ellie emerged from the baby's nursery. She yawned, patted her hair, went downstairs and wandered into the sunroom. To her utter surprise, the table had been set for two. A bud vase held a single yellow rose. The aroma of bacon and fresh biscuits made her mouth water.

Who had set the table for breakfast?

It couldn't have been Caleb. He'd left at dawn to help his father with branding. Besides, Caleb Bentley wasn't the type of man to pick flowers and decorate a breakfast table.

It couldn't have been Ginny. Ellie had given her firm instructions to sleep in this morning. The poor girl had been up several times in the night with a teething child.

That only left one possibility. She crept down the hallway towards the kitchen, stopping in the doorway. She almost gasped at the sight that met her eyes. Niles, her husband, stood at the counter, squeezing oranges.

Lately she was never sure what he'd get up to next. He was a changed man.

Six months prior he'd almost succumbed to pneumonia. The doctors were certain he wouldn't survive, but the stubborn old ox had managed to pull through. To her surprise, she'd rejoiced, and so had he. Since then, they'd been inseparable. He'd sold his overseas holdings and devoted himself to her and their Magnolia family.

She grinned and set her hands on her hips. "Niles Addington, what on earth are you doing?"

Her husband knit his brow but didn't look up. "What does it look like I'm doing?"

"Why are you squeezing oranges?"

"To make orange juice for my bride." He held up an orange rind, accidentally flicking pulp across the counter. "Orange juice *comes* from oranges."

"Aren't you clever."

"Taking care of a toddler is a tremendous joy, wouldn't you say?"

"I would, indeed. Who would have thought the two of us would become such doting grandparents?"

"Joshua was older when we met. I never knew anything about children. I didn't realize they were so delightful." He set his hand over his heart. "Yesterday, little Eleanor called me Pops."

Ellie went to his side. "And because of that, you decided to make breakfast?"

"I wanted to have breakfast with you, so that we could discuss the day. Take the baby for a walk in the new pram, or go with Josh, Sophia and the boys for a picnic."

"So many choices." She leaned closer and kissed his cheek.

He smiled at her and cupped her jaw. In the quiet of the kitchen, they shared a tender gaze as he stroked her cheek. "I love you, Eleanor Addington. With all my heart."

Ellie had learned a lot about love over the past few years. Seeing how happy Caleb made Ginny made her realize how precious time with family was. And when Niles had recovered from his illness, she took that as a second chance at happiness.

She trailed her fingertips along his jaw. "You'd better, Niles Addington."

The End

Brides of Bethany Springs Book One
To Charm a Scarred Cowboy

Texas, 1889 - Daniel Honeycutt is no stranger to peril. His scars are proof. They frighten folks, which is why he prefers a solitary life on his ranch. His long days are a tad lonesome, but at least there's no one around to judge him.

When he sees a girl on a runaway horse, Daniel forgets his scars. His quick thinking saves Molly Collins, and the chance meeting draws Daniel from his solitude.

Molly is unlike any other girl. Headstrong. Impossible. Aggravatingly beautiful. Daniel soon learns Molly is in danger, and he vows to protect her. Even if it means risking his stubborn heart.

Books by Charlotte Dearing

The Bluebonnet Brides Collection
Mail Order Grace
Mail Order Rescue
Mail Order Faith
Mail Order Hope
Mail Order Destiny

Brides of Bethany Springs Series
To Charm a Scarred Cowboy
Kiss of the Texas Maverick
Vow of the Texas Cowboy
The Accidental Mail Order Bride
Starry-Eyed Mail Order Bride
An Inconvenient Mail Order Bride
Amelia's Storm

Mail Order Providence
Mail Order Sarah
Mail Order Ruth

and many others...

Sign up at www.charlottedearing.com to be notified of special offers and announcements.